SPIDER SHEPHERD: SAS

The Sandpit

SPIDER SHEPHERD: SAS

The Sandpit

STEPHEN LEATHER

Dan 'Spider' Shepherd and his SAS team are sent into the badlands of Afghanistan to train rebels who are battling Taliban fanatics. But what starts as a training mission in The Sandpit turns into a life or death struggle with Shepherd and his team very much in the firing line.

And they soon find themselves caught up in an international intrigue that threatens the stability of the whole Middle East. 'The Sandpit' is an action-packed thriller featuring Spider Shepherd during his SAS days, before he signed up as an undercover cop and worked for MI5, written by *Sunday Times* bestselling author Stephen Leather.

CHAPTER 1

D an "Spider" Shepherd glanced around him. The other members of his patrol, Jock McIntyre, Geordie Mitchell and Jimbo Shortt, were almost unrecognisable behind their night vision goggles. They stood poised, weapons at the ready, pressed against a featureless, high brick wall to either side of a locked door. Each of them gave a nod to signal their readiness and Shepherd then held up his gloved left hand and began a silent countdown from five, lowering his fingers one by one. As he reached zero, Jock triggered the frame charge and the door disappeared, blown off its hinges by the force of the explosion.

As the noise of the blast echoed from the surrounding buildings, Shepherd burst through the blackened doorway with his patrol mates at his heels. The building was blacked out, but the green-tinged image through their goggles showed their targets as clearly as if it was bright daylight. Working in pairs, they despatched the targets in the first room with clinical double-taps, then paused for an instant at the doorway to the next to hurl a flash-bang grenade ahead of them. Packed with magnesium and fulminate of mercury, the grenade ignited with a blinding flash, as bright as a 50,000 watt bulb, and a bang so loud that it was guaranteed to disorient anyone who had not been conditioned by constant practice to ignore it.

Shepherd had closed his eyes for an instant and averted his gaze to avoid losing his night vision, but even before the flash had faded he was diving through the doorway. As he hit the floor, he took in the situation in one glance: a row of hostages on chairs at one side of the room with several terrorists guarding them and others stationed at intervals around the rest of the room. Even while his brain was still processing that information, he was already beginning to take out the terrorists with double-taps, firing and then rolling to throw off the aim of any counter-fire, and eliminating the greatest threats first, working outwards from the nearest terrorist to the hostages.

As his gaze took in each potential target in turn, he had a fraction of a second to answer the question: hostage or terrorist? Live or die? A mistaken identification could condemn an innocent hostage to death or allow a terrorist time to kill the hostages or their SAS rescuers, but years of training, practice exercises and actual combat had honed each of the SAS men's fighting skills to such a pitch that there was never a second's hesitation. Shepherd's mind was calm and clear and he was so lacking in tension or nerves that his pulse had barely risen above its resting rate. His gaze flickered onto each fresh target, identified them as friend or foe, and in the same instant his pistol spat twice, the shots so rapid that they sounded like one. Even as the rounds were impacting the target, his attention was already switching to the next target.

The impact followed so close upon each shot that the sounds blurred together: the whipcrack noise as the shot was fired, the wet smack of the impact, triggering a flurry of tiny fibres from the target's balaclava helmet where the round struck home and a corona of larger fragments as it exited through the back, followed by a "thwock", like an echo of the shot, as the round exited the target and penetrated the thick wall-covering behind, and then a faint metallic clang as it struck sheet steel beyond that.

The thunder of gunfire had redoubled within a heartbeat of Shepherd's first double-tap as Jock, Geordie and Jimbo's weapons also spat rounds. They were working to an agreed pattern, so that no terrorist was double-targeted. It would take a terrorist less than a second or two to get their wits together and start shooting their captives. They had to be dead before that could happen.

Unable to see anything in the darkness but the muzzle-flashes as each shot was fired and deafened by the constant drum roll of gunfire, the hostages remained frozen into panic-stricken immobility while a stream of live rounds passed within inches of their bodies. Within seconds, every terrorist target had been eliminated and none of the hostages had so much as a scratch on them. Had one of them been hit, the consequences would have been almost incalculable, but the SAS commanders had such confidence in their men's skills that there was never a moment's hesitation before committing them to action, no matter how difficult the mission might be, and whatever the potential risks they might face. It was what the SAS trained for on a daily basis, training that had them expending thousands of rounds a year.

Shepherd remained prone on the floor for another few moments, his gaze sweeping the room, his Browning pistol still cocked and ready, until a siren sounded and the lights in the room came up. The SAS men got to their feet and stripped off their goggles. They began checking each of the twelve terrorist targets, the dummies positioned at various places in the building, making sure that each had been hit with a double-tap. They then ejected the magazines from their weapons and counted off the rounds fired against the targets hit.

Shepherd smiled as he completed the count. 'We could make it our specialist subject on Mastermind,' he said, 'twenty-four hits and no misses.'

Jock waved away Geordie, the patrol medic, as he tried to carry out his usual post-contact check to see if anyone was wounded. 'We're hardly likely to have been wounded, are we?' Jock said, his rasping Glaswegian accent making him sound even more irritated.

'With your shooting, you never know,' Geordie said with a wink to the others.

Jimbo nudged Shepherd in the ribs and jerked his head towards the seats where the hostages were exchanging nervous small talk with each other. One of them was death-white and still struggling to control a tremor in his hands. 'He looks happy, doesn't he?' said Jimbo.

They heard footsteps behind the sheets of thick, black rubber that hung over every wall and covered the floor, preventing ricochets. So heavy was the use of the Killing House and so intense the rate of firing that the rubber had to be replaced every couple of months. Two of the sheets were held apart and the CO and a party of staff officers and dignitaries who had been watching the demonstration from behind the bullet-proof glass of the observation room in the wall high above them, filed into the room.

The CO inspected the "terrorists", all of which now had two neat holes drilled in the centre of their foreheads, the target area of choice now that the bad guys were starting to wear body armour. He gave a curt nod of approval, then walked across the room to one of the "hostages", who stood up to greet him with a rueful smile on his face. The knees of the man next to him buckled as he began to get up, and he slumped back onto his chair, his face ashen.

'Your Royal Highness,' the CO said. 'I hope you didn't find that too stressful?'

'Not at all,' the Prince said. 'It was the most enormous fun, wasn't it Prime Minister?'

The PM's face still had a deathly pallor, but he forced a feeble smile. 'Indeed it was, Sir.' He made as if to stand up, but then thought better of it and sat down heavily again. 'Though that is probably enough fun for one day,' he added, taking out a handkerchief and mopping the sweat from his brow.

The Prince walked over and shook hands with Shepherd and the other members of the patrol. He had a firm grip and looked them in the eye each time he shook. 'Thank you gentlemen. If I ever do find myself being kidnapped, I now know what to expect! My father did try to tell me what I was in for, but words can't really prepare you for the reality of it, can they?'

'I'm glad you enjoyed it, Sir,' Shepherd said. 'We aim to please.'

'I thought you aimed to kill,' the Prince said, smiling.

'That too,' Shepherd said.

Like his father and grandfather, the Prince always expected and even demanded the full range of formal courtesies from the officers at Hereford, but he seemed much more relaxed and informal around the trogs – the other ranks. They called him 'Sir' the first time they spoke to him, not 'Your Royal Highness', but if there was any further conversation, they didn't use any title at all, but just spoke to him as they would have spoken to each other. Surrounded by sycophants and yes-men in every other area of his life, the Prince seemed to quite like it. However, politicians were another story. The trogs were polite with them, but not over-polite and certainly not deferential, and they didn't call the Prime Minister, 'Sir', in fact they didn't use any title with him at all. SAS troopers tended to have a very low opinion of politicians in general and members of the Cabinet in particular, honed from years of having to clear up their mistakes.

When the Prime Minister's press spokesman challenged the SAS men about their attitude, complaining that they were showing 'a lack of respect for the Prime Minister, who after all, is the man who pays your wages and-.' He was cut off in mid-flow by Jock. 'When we enlisted in the Armed Forces, we took the Queen's Shilling, not the Prime Minister's, and it is the Queen we serve not some jumped up little "here today and gone tomorrow, politician".' He paused, his gaze contemptuous. 'Nor his mouthpiece come to that. You may be able to bully the press, but you'd be well advised not to try it with us. You never know, you might be kidnapped yourself one of these days and while we'd feel obliged to rescue the Prime Minister, I don't think we'd feel quite the same need to risk our lives to save you as well.' His voice was as flat and dispassionate as if he had been discussing the price of a pint of milk, but there was no mistaking the hint of menace behind it. The press spokesman's mouth opened and closed twice without any sound at all emerging from it, and then he turned on his heel and stomped off, taking out his anger on one of the 10 Downing Street underlings, who wasn't quick enough to get out of his way.

While the Prince had been talking to Shepherd, the CO had hovered around them, anxious as ever to divert the royal attention away from the men and back to the officer class. 'As you know, Your Royal Highness,' he said, seizing on a brief pause in the conversation, 'the aim was not to entertain you or scare you witless, but to prepare you for the nightmare scenario. Of course we profoundly hope it will never come to pass, but if we ever do have to stage a genuine rescue, we wouldn't want you jumping up in fright and running into the line of fire.' He paused, and Shepherd hid a smile as he saw the look of panic spreading over the CO's face and the colour rising in his cheeks. 'Not that you look like a man who frightens easily, of course, your Maj- I mean Your Royal Highness.'

Shepherd exchanged a glance with Geordie. 'The CO's even more oleaginous than usual, this morning,' he said out of the side of his mouth.

'Ole-what now?' Geordie said. 'You swallowed a dictionary?'

'It means oily.'

'Then why not say oily?'

'I'm trying to expand your vocabulary, Geordie.'

Geordie grinned. 'What does vocabulary mean again?'

'If I could just interrupt your little chat for a moment?' the CO said, glaring at them.

'Sir?'

'I will escort our distinguished visitors back to the Mess myself, where the Royalty and Diplomatic Protection Groups will re-assume responsibility for their principals. So that will be all. Dismiss.'

'Sir.'

The SAS had trained both the Royalty Protection Group and the Diplomatic Protection Group and whenever a member of the royal family or a politician came to Hereford to take part in a hostage rescue exercise – and it was a trial by ordeal that all senior royals and politicians had to go through – the SAS needed no assistance in protecting them and would have taken it as an insult to their own, much greater expertise. So the bodyguards were always left in the Mess while armed SAS men took responsibility for the safety of their principals. The bodyguards didn't like it one little bit, but that was not a matter of any concern to the SAS men; after all, they were the masters and the RPG and DPG merely their pupils.

Shepherd inclined his head to the Prince and the Prime Minister, and was starting to lead his patrol out of the Killing House, when the CO called out to him. 'By the way, there will be a briefing for an op at 1800 hours.'

'Sir.'

'Well that was fun, but it's still no match for the real thing,' Jimbo said, as they filed out into the usual

Hereford drizzle and stood on the gritty tarmac surrounding the Killing House.

Geordie grinned. 'Did you see the Prime Minister's face? He wasn't just pale, he was green around the gills. I was sure he was going to throw up.'

'Yeah, HRH handled it pretty well,' Jimbo said, 'but the PM was absolutely shitting himself.'

'If it was up to me, I'd make any politician who orders our troops into action spend a week on the front line, just so they can see what war is actually like,' said Shepherd. 'For them war is just charts and statistics, they'd look at it differently if the bullets were flying their way.' He grinned. 'And yeah, it was nice to wipe that shit-eating smile from his face for once.'

Jock had been glancing around while they were talking. 'Every time I come out of the Killing House I still think there's something missing. I just haven't got used to the chapel not being here,' he said, gesturing to the cleared site where the Regimental chapel had once stood. By a quirk of Army logic that no one had ever been able adequately to explain, the chapel had originally been sited right next door to the Killing House. 'They want the shortest walk for the coffin-bearers if anything goes wrong,' had been Jock's best explanation for it at the time, but since Sunday was just another working day to SAS men, the result was that church services had always taken place to a background of thuds, bangs and explosions. When the old wooden camp was rebuilt and remodelled, the chapel had been moved to a different site, though since it now backed on to the main railway line between Hereford and Newport, its new location didn't really suggest any greater respect for the sanctity of church services.

'I don't know why it bothers you,' Shepherd said. 'The only time you've ever been inside the bloody chapel in all the years you've been in the Regiment is when you've been there for a funeral.'

Jock shrugged. 'Maybe, but God knows there has been no shortage of those over the years, so I've still spent quite a bit of time in there.'

'God knows?'

'It's an expression. It doesn't mean I believe.'

Shepherd grinned. 'Geordie, mate, I've never yet met a soldier who doesn't ask God for help when he's under fire.'

Geordie nodded. 'Always best to cover all your bases,' he said. 'Inshalla.'

Shepherd chuckled as he checked his watch. 'Anyway, I'd love to stand around here talking shite with you three for another hour or two but I'd better go and get my kit sorted. If we're briefing at six we might be on our way tonight.'

'Where do you think we'll be heading this time?' asked Jimbo.

'We'll find out soon enough, but I tell you what, I'll be packing my thermal underwear. You don't have to be psychic to work it out, do you? Afghanistan's the only game in town at the moment. We're off to the Sandpit, no question.'

Geordie nodded. 'Especially now winter's nearly over and the fighting season is about to fire up again.'

'It's what those Afghans do best,' Jock said. 'But then again, they've been practising for about 150 years, so I suppose they ought to be quite good at it by now.'

'You never know, I might even get another crack at Muj 1 as well,' Shepherd said. 'They owe me that much.'

'Give it a rest, Spider,' Jock said. 'Change the record will you? Yes, we know, you had bin Laden in your sights at the Tora Bora caves, and the Head Shed wouldn't let you make the shot 'cos the Yanks wanted the glory for themselves.'

'And as usual they fucked up.'

'Yeah, we know that too,' Geordie said wearily, pushing his fingers through his thinning hair. 'You're like a broken record sometimes, Spider. Just let Muj 1 go. It's not like we're short of targets, is it?'

'Well, I'm just saying, if I ever get another chance to slot him, I won't be asking the Head Shed for clearance. I'll be shooting first and only asking if it's all right with them when I can see bits of his brains spread all over those godforsaken mountains the Afghans call home.'

Jock rolled his eyes 'And I'm just saying that if I hear any more about Muj 1, it won't be his brains that are in danger of being used as pebble-dash.'

'Anyway, I don't know about Muj 1,' Geordie said, 'but I'd say we'll definitely be seeing a bit more of those mountains, probably a lot more than we'd like. But at least we'll be shooting at the real thing.'

'See you at 1800 then,' Shepherd said, walking away across the car park. It had once been the parade ground, but that had always been by far the least used part of the base, since the SAS had never been big on drill, marching and parades, and eventually part of it had been turned into a car park and the rest, marked by a huge white circle with "H" in the middle of it, was a part-time helipad.

Shepherd paused, as he always did, when he passed the regimental clock. Paid for by the contributions of every serving SAS man at the time, who had all contributed a day's pay to cover the cost, the plinth at its foot bore the names of all those who had died in training or on active service with the Regiment. Shepherd didn't have to count them to know that there were now well over 100 names on it, including that of his best mate Liam. He had drowned on a training exercise off the Norwegian coast that their CO – a different one, a medal-chasing glory hog who was ever willing to volunteer his men for anything and everything that would boost his ego and his reputation with his superiors – had recklessly insisted on staging despite being urged by the navy and the coastguard to call it off because of an approaching storm. Shepherd felt his anger flaring once more at the thought and had to push it away as he strode on.

He hurried back to the house he shared with his wife Sue and their young son, Liam, named for

Shepherd's lost friend. He hesitated with his hand on the door handle, composing his features before he went in. He knew that Sue wasn't going to be happy to hear that he was heading off again. Liam heard the door and came running from the kitchen and hugged his dad around the knees until Shepherd picked him up and carried him through to the kitchen where Sue was at the stove. 'You're early,' she said. 'Should I be pleased or worried?' She turned and smiled though Shepherd could sense her unease.

He kissed her on the lips. 'Probably both at once,' he said. 'We've got a briefing at six and I've got an uneasy feeling it isn't just to tell us what a good job we made of scaring the Prime Minister shitless this afternoon.'

She stopped what she was doing and turned to face him. 'Another mission? Already? Are you serious? You've only just got back.'

'Honey, I'm sorry. But that's what we signed up for.'

'I know, I know,' she said, her voice weary. 'But it wasn't what I signed up for.'

Shepherd was tempted to disagree, but if his years of marriage and the regular arguments about the competing demands of the SAS and his family had taught him anything, it was that sometimes the wisest reply was no reply at all, and he remained silent.

'What are you cooking?'

'Nice change of subject,' she said.

'It smells good.'

'It's just a bolognaise sauce,' she said. 'I'm doing lasagne.'

'My favourite.'

She laughed despite herself. 'It's not your bloody favourite and you know it. I just wanted something that would keep in the oven because I didn't know how long you'd be.' She forced a smile. 'You're back earlier than I thought. I can do the lasagne for the freezer and cook you a steak.'

'A steak sounds good.'

'You play with Liam while I cook, he doesn't see anywhere near enough of you.'

'I was wondering if we should maybe get started on a little sister or brother for Liam.'

Sue frowned. 'What?'

'You know what I mean. He'd be happier with a brother or sister, right?'

'That's your plan? You're always away so a sibling will fill the gap?'

'Is that such a bad idea?'

She sighed. 'No, it's not a bad idea. Not if we were a normal family. But I'm dealing with Liam on my own most of the time and I'm not sure I could handle two.'

'I hear you,' said Shepherd. He nuzzled his son and Liam giggled. 'Looks like you're going to have to wait a while, Liam,' he said.

'Or you could get yourself a regular job,' said Sue.

'Nine to Five?'

'Would that be so bad?' she asked, turning to face him. 'A job where I knew when you'd walk through the door and where you didn't disappear for weeks at a time?'

'I'm not sure I'm ready for that,' he said. 'I'm sorry. Is it that bad?'

She shrugged. 'You're the man I married,' she said. 'I knew what I was getting into.' She smiled. 'I love you, for better or worse. And I am proud of you. How many husbands get to hang out with the Prime Minister and a prince of the realm?'

'Not many, that's true.' He kissed her on the lips again. 'Steak sounds great. Liam and I will be doing some father-son bonding in front of the TV.'

As he left for the briefing that evening, Sue clung to him for a long moment, and he could feel her tears wetting his neck. 'It's worse every time you go away. Please be careful.'

'Being careful doesn't tend to sit too well with being in the Regiment, but I'll do my best.' He kissed her, hugged Liam a final time and then hurried away, pausing to raise a hand in farewell as he reached the corner of the street.

CHAPTER 2

Shepherd and his patrol mates proved to be fifty per cent right about the briefing that evening. The destination of the next operation was indeed the Sandpit. Afghanistan. Their mission was to link up with mujahideen fighters loyal to the memory of Ahmad Shah Massoud before moving by road to the Panjshir Valley. Ahmad Shah Massoud, known as 'The Lion of Panjshir', was the leader of Jamiat-e Islami – the Northern Alliance, or the United Islamic Front for the Salvation of Afghanistan, to give it its proper title. Until he was assassinated in September 2001, Massoud was the political and military leader who led the resistance to the Soviet occupation between 1979 and 1989 and the years of civil war that followed.

The plan was for the SAS to spend the summer fighting season there, training the junior officers of the late Massoud's fighters in small unit Special Forces tactics. They left Hereford that night, though they didn't head to Afghanistan right away. As was standard practice once a "Warning Order" for an imminent active service operation had been given to them, they were transferred to the SAS's purpose-built isolation camp away from the main base, Stirling Lines, for an intensive period of work-up training.

Everything they could conceivably need to help them prepare for the operation – equipment, weapons, explosives, firing ranges – was already in place at the camp, with a dedicated support team to take care of any administration, so that the patrol was free to concentrate one hundred per cent on the task in hand. They spent the next fortnight training relentlessly, building up their already considerable stamina to an even higher pitch and practising their skills, including long sessions in the Close Quarter Battle area. They studied large scale maps and surveillance imagery from aircraft and satellite over-flights to familiarise themselves with the terrain in which they would be operating. They also ate like starving men, trying to add a few pounds, since they knew that they would struggle for adequate rations to replace the calories they would be burning while inside Afghanistan and would inevitably lose weight. Jock, the old man of the patrol, was an old Afghan hand, having helped to train the mujahideen fighters of Ahmad Shah Massoud's Northern Alliance, which had fought, almost alone, against the Taliban as they swept to power in Afghanistan. Shepherd, Geordie and Jimbo had only spent a few months in country before, most notably during the abortive pursuit of Osama bin Laden that was still causing Shepherd so much anger and so many sleepless nights.

At the end of their fortnight's work-up training, they were not driven to RAF Odiham, home base of the newly formed Joint Special Forces Aviation Wing, where the SAS could draw on Chinook and Lynx helicopters and fixed wing aircraft flown by the cream of the RAF's pilots. Instead they were taken to RAF Lyneham, where the RAF's fleet of C-130 Hercules transports was based. They flew out that night on one of the noisy and draughty Hercs, for the long, ear-numbing flight to Islamabad in Pakistan. They arranged themselves among their kit and rucksacks and sprawled on the bare aluminium floor. Their cover as part of an NGO team helping with water and medical aid meant that they couldn't take firearms with them, something none of them was happy about. As usual Shepherd remained awake, staring into space, thinking about the mission ahead and the family he had left behind. As usual Jock and Geordie had curled up on the floor and fallen instantly asleep. Shepherd had long envied them their ability to sleep anywhere, anytime, no matter how noisy and uncomfortable, but try as he might, he was never able to do so himself. Jimbo sat in a jump seat, reading the latest Andy McNab book and occasionally laughing out loud.

When they landed in Islamabad, they were hustled straight through security and driven to the British High Commission, where they were kitted out with a full range of civilian equipment and clothing, all of which was deliberately non-military in appearance and origin, together with documents supporting their cover story that they were in Pakistan to work for a Non-Governmental Organisation. Unusually the patrol would not be taking a radio transmitter with them. Instead they would each carry a world band transistor receiver with which they could listen on pre-set frequencies using the British Forces Broadcasting Service to receive instructions from Hereford. Just like Second World War BBC broadcasts that contained coded messages to agents operating in Occupied France, instructions to the SAS men would be broadcast during normal BFBS programmes in codes and phrases which only the patrol and SAS HQ would be able to decipher. The patrol signaller, Jimbo, was carrying a few pages of a one time pad code book inside a bag armed with a strong acid solution. In the event of being compromised or close to capture he could destroy the code book in seconds.

The High Commissioner proved to be a relatively junior career diplomat, an almost impossibly young-looking official, with a cut-glass accent and a tweed jacket that was not only wildly inappropriate in the subtropical heat and humidity of Islamabad, but also marked him out as the sort of public school and Oxbridge 'chap' that the FCO still tended to recruit, despite their protestations of equal opportunities for all. He also appeared to be fulfilling the FCO's traditional policy for its up and coming diplomats – a couple of early postings at what they described as 'challenging' postings – or 'shitholes' as Jock rather more accurately described them. Only later, providing he had kept his nose clean and avoided upsetting any of the FCO mandarins along the way, would he be given his reward – an ambassadorial post at one of the more desirable embassies, perhaps one of the minor European capitals. Ultimately, if all went well and he was judged the right material – a sufficiently clubbable chap – he might hope to cap his career with a stint in one of the most keenly coveted roles, as ambassador in Paris, Beijing, Moscow, the UN or even Washington. Gongs and a knighthood would inevitably follow. But that was down the line – Shepherd and his team had to deal with a young, inexperienced diplomat who was clearly out of his depth.

The High Commissioner clearly couldn't wait to get rid of them and passed them along to one of the resident FCO spooks, an SIS – aka MI6 – officer working undercover as an attaché in the High Commission. He said his name was Ralph Nelson, but that was almost certainly a lie. MI6 officers rarely used their real names. He was an earnest young ex-cavalry officer, blue-eyed and blond-haired, new into the SIS and evidently very keen. There was a gleam in his eye and the colour rose to his cheeks as he began outlining the background to their mission. 'I won't underplay the difficulties of this operation,' he said, sounding like it was the most exciting thing he'd ever heard of. 'Pakistan's ISI continues to support the Taliban, more or less openly. They fund their operations and also act as a conduit for funds from Saudi Arabia and elsewhere in the Middle East. They supply or facilitate the supply of weapons, ammunition and fuel, train Taliban fighters and act as an entry point for recruits arriving from all over the Muslim world. They have also planned and directed Taliban offensives, provided military and logistical support including air strikes, and have sent regular troops from their own army to fight alongside the Taliban. And best of all, in November 2001, just as we had them cornered, Pakistan flew the Taliban and al Qaeda leaders, and their own ISI operatives out of Kunduz in Afghanistan to their bases at Chitral and Gilgit, and then gave them safe haven in the Tribal Areas.

'Yeah, we heard about that,' Geordie said. 'The flight of shame.'

Nelson flashed him a tight smile before continuing. 'Within Afghanistan there are more factions than you can shake a shitty stick at. Like every Muslim country, it is divided along religious lines between Sunni and Shia, but that's just the start of it, because there are also a multitude of rival ethnic groupings including Pushtuns, Tajiks, Uzbeks, Hazaris and Turkomen. There are thousands of Pakistani "volunteers" – though many of them are believed to be moonlighting regular soldiers of the Pakistan army – and the Chechens, Arabs and other Sunni volunteers recruited by al Qaeda. The situation is confused and hostilities are continuing between the various Afghan factions, all of which form alliances that are constantly shifting, so your enemy today becomes your friend tomorrow and then your enemy again by the end of the week. The original loose cannon warlord, Gulbuddin Hekmatyar, is also still out there, and he's willing to fight anyone and everyone if the price is right. The Saudis are still bankrolling al Qaeda and at least one of the rival Sunni factions and, although the Iranians supplied us with intelligence that helped to topple the Taliban, like everyone else they are pursing their own vested interests and are actively supporting one of the Shia factions. Russia, India, Turkey and Tajikistan are also busy in Afghanistan in pursuit of their own interests.'

'Bloody hell,' Jimbo said. 'It all sounds like a classic cluster-fuck. So whose side are we on…for the moment, anyway?'

'We're supporting the new regime in Kabul, the legitimate government of Afghanistan,' said Nelson earnestly.

Jock laughed. 'The legitimate government once the Yanks had installed it, you mean. Karzai's about as legitimate as a seventeen-pound note and as straight as a snake going up a sand dune.'

Nelson's lips pursed. 'Nonetheless, he is our ally and our role here is to support his regime and give it sufficient security to allow an orderly progress to full democracy.' He sounded as if he was reading from a script.

Jock gave another derisive snort. He was several years older than the other patrol members, but his

argumentative nature and short fuse under provoca-
tion had led to him being busted back down to the
ranks twice after settling disputes with fellow-soldiers
with his fists. Had the men he'd punched been officers rather than other NCOs and had he not been
such a brilliant soldier, he would almost certainly
have been RTU'd – dismissed from the Regiment
and sent back to his original unit – but the SAS had
always valued military effectiveness more than social
airs and graces and good manners, and there was no
more effective soldier than Jock.

However, even the SAS's patience was not limit-
less and Jock was now on a final warning, so Shepherd
intervened before the argument could escalate. 'OK,
you can spare us the political and moral justifica-
tion for supporting Karzai,' he said to Nelson, while
shooting a warning look at Jock. 'We're just pulling
your chain a little. We're soldiers. We follow orders.
Tell us to jump, we'll just say "How high?" End of
story. So what else do we need to know?'

Nelson smiled gratefully before continuing. 'The
new regime's control of much of the country is still
fragile at best and they're almost entirely dependent
on the support of ourselves and the Americans,' he
said. 'So, since the Taliban have not gone away, and
are regrouping with the help of the Pakistani ISI,
we're also supporting any faction strong enough to
resist a resurgent Taliban, and that mainly means
what's left of the Northern Alliance.'

'Because our enemy's enemy, is our friend, right?' said Shepherd.

'They're a pretty bloodthirsty bunch – but then you probably wouldn't want to be taken prisoner by any of the factions – but they're the best of a bad lot,' said Nelson. He paused. 'However, there's something else in play too, because there has been a sudden escalation recently. Signals intercepts are running at about twice the normal rate, the rumour mills in the Tribal Areas are in overdrive, and the flow of men and material crossing into Afghanistan has dramatically increased.'

'Isn't that normal at the start of the fighting season?' Shepherd said, frowning.

'It is, but the level of activity now is far above the normal rate at this time of year,' said Nelson. 'So your task is to make your way to a safe house in Peshawar, where you will link up with a group of Afghan mujahideen fighters from the Panjshir Valley, which is where Massoud came from. He was a Tajik and a Sunni Muslim, and his men were mostly fellow-Tajiks, Uzbeks and Hazaras, whereas of course the Taliban and the majority of Afghans are Pushtuns. There's no love lost between them, obviously. Ahmad Shah Massoud was the only mujahideen leader not to leave Afghanistan during the war with the Soviets and he was also the only one to fight to defend his territory when the Taliban swept to power. He had pretty much defeated the might of the Soviet army and fought the

Taliban to a standstill, but he was then killed by two suicide bombers. You know the story, right?'

Shepherd nodded but the rest of the team shook their heads. 'The bombers gained access to him by posing as television reporters,' Nelson explained. 'Then they detonated a bomb concealed in a video camera, blew themselves and their target to bits. Shortly before that occurred, Massoud had been warning his Western allies that al Qaeda was planning an imminent large-scale attack on US soil, and it's possible that his murder was in retaliation for that. It's probably not without significance that he was killed on 9 September 2001, just two days before the 9/11 attacks on the World Trade Centre.'

'Bastards,' muttered Jock under his breath.

Nelson paused before resuming with a brisker tone. 'So, some of his mujahideen followers will be your escorts as you cross into Afghanistan. Their job is to take you to meet the heirs to the legend, deep in the Panjshir Valley. Your job is to train them in Special Forces methods and tactics so they can take the fight to the Taliban and any other factions seeking to destabilise the regime.'

'You know we didn't come with weapons,' said Shepherd.

'I've got my knife,' said Jimbo.

Shepherd flashed him a warning look before continuing. 'Our cover is working for an NGO so we were told no weapons.'

'Well, obviously,' said Nelson. 'If anything were to go wrong the last thing we want is for British Army equipment to be paraded on TV. You can pick up anything you need locally, there's a lot of Russian stuff around which will muddy the waters somewhat should anything...'

He was going to say 'go wrong' but he left the sentence unfinished and just shrugged.

'And how long are we here for?' asked Shepherd.

'As long as it takes,' said Nelson. 'Don't get me wrong, these guys are hardened fighters already. But we need to give them that little bit extra. Right survival brief. If Escape and Evasion becomes necessary there is plentiful drinking water everywhere in Afghanistan except for the south-western deserts, but even in the high mountains it is likely to be contaminated so you must use your Puritabs to sterilise it. Food should not be too difficult to find on the plains and in the foothills, where there are wheat fields, rice paddies and plenty of fruit and nut trees.'

'Don't be daft,' Jock said, 'everyone knows Cadbury's fruit and nut doesn't grow on trees.'

The others grinned while Nelson pursed his lips in annoyance, but battled on. 'There are also several different kinds of grapes, almonds, walnuts, mulberries, pomegranates and stone fruit including apricots.'

'And since this is the end of winter, none of the foodstuffs you've mentioned will be available to us at this time of year, nor for at least three months from now,' Jimbo said. 'Isn't there anything more useful you can tell us?'

'Then try this instead,' Nelson said, once more failing to conceal his irritation. 'If you need to E&E overland, you will find that Afghanistan is one of the worst countries in the world from which to do so, both for natural and political reasons. There are deserts to the south and west of the country, as I've said, and the borders in all other directions are very mountainous. If you do manage to cross them, you will find that without exception, every one of the surrounding countries is Muslim and most of them have at least some loyalty to the Taliban. You shouldn't expect a welcome in any of the former Soviet republics, nor in Iran, and if you did manage to reach the Chinese frontier – and since it lies beyond the very highest mountain ranges that is not very likely, you will find that the indigenous population there are also sympathetic to the Taliban. So Pakistan is probably the best option, but as I'm sure you're aware, the Pakistani government and its agencies, while officially allies of ours, are unofficially supporting the Taliban too.'

'It's all right, lad,' said Jock. 'We've all read Bravo Two Zero, we know how to get out of sticky situations.'

Nelson frowned, not sure if Jock was being serious or not. Shepherd flashed Jock a warning look. Banter was all well and good among the troops but in his experience MI6 officers didn't have much in the way of a sense of humour.

Nelson paused again, putting the tips of his fingers together and furrowing his brow in concentration before he continued. 'Just one more thing,' he said, 'and I must stress that this is my own personal view, and definitely not that of Her Majesty's Government. Someone is stirring up the whole region and, though I've no hard evidence to back this up, I suspect that it is part of an attempt by the Iranians to get their hands on Pakistan's nuclear secrets. Unfortunately, no one else here or in London buys into the theory, but the whole area is in turmoil and the population is once more breaking down into conflicting factions along tribal and religious grounds. It's always been a dangerous place but now it's more perilous then ever, and the area around the Panjshir Valley is the most dangerous of all. So please watch out for yourselves, because no one else is going to.'

'So just to be clear, you won't be sending James Bond in to haul our nuts out of the fire if it all turns to shit?' asked Geordie. Nelson and Shepherd both glared at Geordie and he raised his hands in apologetic surrender. 'Okay, okay, I was just trying to lighten the moment,' he said.

As they walked down the corridor from the spook's office, Shepherd glanced around at the other members of the patrol. 'So, what do you make of that, guys?'

'It's a wee bit scary,' Jock said. 'He might just be a bit of a Hooray Henry who thinks he is playing Kipling's Great Game, but on the other hand, he could just be right. And the fact that his bosses don't buy into his theory doesn't make it any less credible.'

'He does seem to know his stuff,' Geordie said, 'not like his bosses because we all know that they don't know their arses from their elbows.'

There was a rumble of agreement from the others; they had all had previous bitter experience of the incompetence of MI6.

'So like he said, we need to watch out for ourselves because no one else will,' said Shepherd.

'No change there then,' growled Jock.

CHAPTER 3

After leaving the High Commission, Shepherd and his team collected the rest of their kit and were then driven back to the airport where they boarded a decrepit looking aircraft for the short hop to the border town of Peshawar. The Peshawar airport was bustling with a very unusual feature – a railway line that crossed one end of the main runway.

'Bloody hell,' Geordie said, when he caught sight of a goods train clanking its way along the line, after they had got off the plane and were walking across the cracked concrete towards the terminal. 'I'm glad I didn't know about that before we came into land. I'd have been shitting myself that we were about to plough into the Khyber express as we landed.'

An army driver, dressed like a local, met them inside the terminal, a drab and suffocatingly hot concrete structure. Above their heads slowly-turning ceiling fans barely offered any detectable current of air and did little to disturb the squadrons of flies circling around them. The driver ushered them out of a side entrance of the terminal and drove them into Peshawar in an unmarked Toyota. They shoved their kitbags into the boot then Shepherd got into the front seat and the three others squeezed into the back with Jimbo in the middle. They passed along Khyber Road, through the ugly urban sprawl to the west of the town. It was punctuated at intervals by buildings from the British colonial heyday, including a mock-Gothic church and a red-brick replica of a Norman castle, complete with battlemented towers guarding the gate. A sign proclaimed that this was the headquarters of the Frontier Police.

'Very picturesque,' Jimbo said, 'but I'm not sure that battlements would have much of a deterrent effect on twenty-first century terrorists. I think berms, concrete blocks and anti-blast shields would offer a lot better protection.'

'You should suggest that to them,' said Jock.

Further on they passed an even more curious structure, like a Hollywood version of a Grecian temple, complete with Doric columns, a triangular pediment and an inscription on the facade reading "Cantt Board".

'What's a Cantt?' Geordie said, gesturing at the lettering.

'You're a Cantt,' said Jimbo, quick as a flash and they all laughed.

The driver smiled for the first time. He hadn't said a word since they'd climbed into the car, Shepherd assumed he was a bit overawed being in the presence of the SAS. 'It's short for Cantonment,' he said. 'It was laid out by the Brits in the 19th century to house the military garrison when Peshawar was the head-quarters of the North-West Frontier, guarding the approaches to the Khyber Pass.'

They drove on, past the massive walls of the old city towering above them, but then ground to a halt in the teeming traffic blocking the roads. They inched past heavy-laden, smoke belching lorries making for the Khyber Pass, jostling for space with pushbikes groaning under the weight of goods piled on the handlebars and saddles, motorbikes and battered saloons. There were also hordes of Qingqi motorised rickshaws, motorbikes with a cramped, covered two-wheeled trailer replacing the motorbike's back wheel and capable of housing six or even more passengers, squashed into the tiny seats. The traffic noise was deafening, a cacophony of blaring horns and revving engines, and a brown haze of pollution hung over the whole of the city.

'Bloody hell,' Jock said, wrinkling his nose. 'This place stinks worse than the Gorbals.'

They eventually emerged from the worst of the traffic jams and soon afterwards the driver turned in through a gateway set in the high walls of the safe house in the heart of the old city where they would be temporarily based. The walls surrounding the property were of mud brick on the outside, match-ing the neighbouring houses, but on the inside, they had been strengthened with brick and reinforced concrete. The house had carved wooden doors and shutters, and an ornate, latticed wooden balcony, and was surrounded by a large garden shaded by mulberry trees.

'This isn't bad at all,' Geordie said as they unloaded their kit. 'Have we got the place to ourselves?'

'All yours,' the driver said, 'apart from a group of Scaleybacks from the British Diplomatic Signals Unit.'

'They were here when I was in Peshawar two years ago,' Jock said. 'They receive messages from inside the Panjshir and then relay them to the High Commission and the Foreign and Commonwealth Office in London. Just about everybody in Peshawar knew they were here but the concept of "plausible denial" allowed Her Majesty's Principal Secretary of State for Foreign and Commonwealth Affairs back in London to stand up in the House of Commons and tell Parliament, straight-faced, that no direct support was being given by the British Government to the mujahideen in Afghanistan.'

'That's not an outright lie though,' said Shepherd. 'They just pass messages, they don't actually fight.'

Jock laughed. 'Fair point,' he said. 'When was the last time you saw a Scaleyback with a gun in his hand?'

'I'm to leave you here,' said the driver. 'Good luck and all.'

They watched him get back into the car and drive away, then turned to look at the house again. They realised they were being watched by a bearded man in a tunic and baggy trousers, sitting on the porch of a house some distance away. By his side was an AK-47 with a folding stock,

'Is the gun a bad sign, do you think?' growled Jock.

'Any male over twelve has a weapon out here,' said Shepherd.

The man waved and Shepherd waved back. Then he stood up, slung his AK-47 over his shoulder and walked towards them.

Jimbo reached for his knife but Shepherd shook his head. 'If he was going to shoot us he'd have done it already. I think he's the guy we're here to see.'

Shepherd was right. The man was the boss of the mujahideen tribesmen who would be forming their escort as they made their way across the border and deep into Afghanistan to the Panjshir Valley. He was in his thirties with a hooked nose and piercing brown eyes. He smiled showing flawless teeth, then introduced himself in near-flawless English. 'I am Ahmad,' he said. 'I was named after my uncle, Ahmad Shah Massoud, and I fight on against the Taliban in his name.'

'Your uncle was a true warrior,' said Shepherd. 'A lion murdered by jackals.'

Ahmad nodded. 'Thank you for that, my friend,' he said.

Shepherd introduced him to the others. 'You speak very good English,' he said.

'I've been living in the UK for the last year,' Ahmad said. 'I was sent there to learn English. It is wise to know the language of our allies, because very few of them can speak ours. I say allies, some would say occupiers.'

Shepherd inclined his head at the implied rebuke.

'Anyway, I was on my way back from the UK,' Ahmad said, 'when I was asked if I and my men would escort a small group of British Army trainers who were coming to the Panjshir to teach us how to fight. I am guessing that would be you.' He gave a mirthless smile. 'And yet that is something we have been doing quite successfully for generations.' He shrugged. 'Ask your dead ancestors, Englishmen, and they will tell you how well Afghans can fight.'

Shepherd saw Jimbo bristling and hastily cut him off. 'No one doubts the Afghans' courage and fighting skill, Ahmad, but they're often not that well organised, militarily speaking. We're no braver than you and your men, but we are more professional and we're here to teach you ways to fight even more effectively. We're just here to teach you some techniques that you might find useful.'

'I meant no offence,' Ahmad said, bowing his head. 'But my men were asking if the West thought we were lacking as fighters.'

'That's absolutely not the case,' said Shepherd. 'Everyone remembers how your men sent the Russians running away with their tails between their legs.'

Ahmad nodded. 'I hope so,' he said. 'Anyway, we are grateful for whatever help you can offer us and you will find that we are quick learners. So the sooner we begin our journey, the sooner we can begin the training, and in fact we must not delay but get moving as quickly as possible. The bazaars are full of rumours and my uncle needs us with him.'

'Your uncle?' Shepherd said. 'I'm confused. I thought Ahmad Shah Massoud had been killed.'

'He was, Allah Yusallimuh, may God bless him and may he rest with the Prophet. But he had five brothers. One of them is my father and the other four of them are, of course, my uncles, including the one who is now our leader.'

'So how do you propose getting there?' Shepherd said. 'It's obviously not safe to go by road.'

'No it isn't, but we can go the old ways, on foot through the mountains, by-passing Kabul altogether. We will travel secretly, mostly by night, and avoid any other travellers, just like we did in the days of the Russians. Inshallah.'

'Inshallah doesn't cut it for me,' said Jock. 'It's not about God being willing. We are going to have to wait a while before setting out, because we can't move until the high mountain passes are clear of the winter snows.' He intercepted Ahmad's quizzical look. 'I may not be an Afghan, but I do know what I'm talking about because I walked to the Panjshir Valley along this route a couple of years ago. I actually set off a month later than this and even then it was right hairy up above the snow-line.'

'We will set off when we feel it is right to do so,' Ahmad said. 'Inshallah.' He grinned. 'Don't worry, Englishmen, we will keep you safe.'

'I'm not worried,' Jock said, 'and even more important, not only am I not an Englishman but I don't need you to keep me safe either.'

Ahmad frowned. 'You're not English?'

'I'm no more English than you're a Pakistani,' said Jock. 'I'm Scottish.'

'A proud warrior race, but they tend to have short fuses,' said Geordie. 'And even shorter dicks.'

'Scottish,' said Ahmad. He nodded. 'I will remember that.'

'What you need to remember is that only a fool would try to cross the mountains when the passes are completely blocked with snow,' said Jock. He paused, and when he spoke again, his tone was more sympathetic. 'Listen Ahmad, we know you're worried about what's going on at home, but setting off now would be too dangerous.'

Ahmad's eyes were cold but he nodded. 'We can wait,' he said, then turned and walked away back to his house.

'Try not to piss off the locals, Jock,' said Shepherd. 'Hearts and minds, remember?'

CHAPTER 4

While the SAS men waited for the snows to melt, Ahmad and his men went to the bazaar in the centre of Peshawar every day and talked to the traders, merchants and lorry drivers who had travelled through the Khyber Pass that day, sifting the gossip and rumour for news from the Panjshir Valley, and every day they seemed even more concerned on their return. Shepherd and his men felt their own concerns increasing as they saw the mujahideen becoming ever more unsettled and edgy. 'We must go soon,' Ahmad said. 'There have been attacks on our people. Only yesterday a village was attacked.'

Shepherd made a non-committal response, all too well aware of how treacherous the mountains could be in the winter, and Ahmad and his men went back to their house, clearly disgruntled.

'They must be communicating with the Panjshir by telepathy,' Jimbo said when they were alone again. 'They're not getting the information through the Scaleybacks, that's for sure, and even the Afghan rumour mill can't be working that fast.'

'Whether it's telepathy, an Ouija board or divine intervention,' Shepherd said, 'we've all noticed the tension in the air ourselves when we've been walking through the bazaar. You could cut the atmosphere with a knife. Something is going on and I'd say it's about to kick off in a big way.'

Over the next couple of days things grew increasingly edgy. Ahmad was constantly annoying the signallers by pestering them for more news from the Panjshir Valley.

Jock knew Ahmad by reputation from his previous visit to the Panjshir, but now he was seriously concerned about the man's behaviour. 'I was always told that Ahmad was a really laid-back, phlegmatic character,' he said to Shepherd. 'But that's certainly not the way he's acting now. Something isn't right. Ahmad must know full well that we can't even think about moving until the passes are clear. I reckon that something is definitely about to go bang.'

A couple of days later, Shepherd and the others were sitting in the garden of the safe house, soaking up the spring sunshine, when Ahmad emerged from his house. He walked towards them and then hovered nearby, his AK-47 slung over his shoulder. 'Whatever is on your mind, Ahmad,' Shepherd said, 'spit it out.'

Ahmad hesitated for a few more seconds and then said 'It is time. There is more fighting in the Panjshir. We are needed there to defend our families and our homes. We will leave at dawn tomorrow, whether or not the mountain passes are clear.'

'But it's madness to set off now,' Jock said, 'we could easily freeze to bloody death out there. And when I went in last time we had donkeys and horses to carry our kit, whereas at this time of year, even if we do manage to get over the passes, we are going to have to back-pack absolutely everything.

'We don't care,' said Ahmad. 'My men have decided. I am their leader but I cannot overrule their wishes, even if I wanted to. Families come first.'

'We could all die up there,' said Jock.

'Only cowards would allow their families to perish because they were worried about the terrain,' said Ahmad.

'I'm not a fucking coward, mate,' snapped Jock. 'You watch your fucking mouth.'

'I did not say you were a coward,' said Ahmad patiently. 'But my men want to go now. And I will go with them. Whether you come or not is down to you. If you don't want to go, I understand, It isn't your families that are at risk.'

Both men looked to Shepherd for a decision. 'Ahmad, do you swear to me that it is safe to leave now?' he said. 'Because getting stuck in the snow out on the mountains and freezing to death is not going to help your families, is it? Would we not be better waiting a few more days for the weather to break? Our met guys are talking about a thaw soon.'

Ahmad's lips were set in a thin line. 'If we wait for the spring thaw, the rivers will be impassable and our families may well have been killed by the time we get there. Now is the time, we must leave at dawn.'

Shepherd thought for a few more seconds, then looked up, squaring his shoulders. 'I reckon that it's either now or never,' he said at last. 'Whether we like it or not, we've got to go. If the passes are too tough for us, they will be too tough for anyone who might be trying to follow us or be lying in wait for us.'

Jock looked about to say something else but, having checked the expressions of Geordie and Jimbo, he then spread his hands in a gesture of surrender. 'All right, maybe it's for the best anyway, all this hanging around waiting for something to happen is driving me crazy.'

'There's one more thing I think we should attend to before we go,' Shepherd said. 'The atmosphere around here is telling me that we may need to modify our preparations a little, so I for one am going to go down to the bazaar and try to get my hands on a bit more hardware.'

'You can count us all in on that,' Jimbo said. 'I'll feel a lot happier carrying something that packs a bit more punch than a naan bread and a packet of raisins.'

'We've got a choice of two souqs,' Jock said. 'The Karkhanai Bazaar, the Smugglers' Market, a few clicks west of town, apparently sells everything from bolt action rifles from around the time of the First

World War and AK-47s nicked from Soviet soldiers in the 1980s, right up to American M-16s liberated from the warehouses and weapon stores in Afghanistan during the last few months. The one thing that everything there has in common is the fact that it has all been nicked from somewhere or other. Or if you fancy something a little more exotic, we can head south for half an hour and give ourselves a real treat: the bazaar at Darra Adam Khel near Kohat, which is famous throughout the Middle East for the range of weaponry that is on sale there. They don't just sell arms, they manufacture them too, and all by hand. I've heard it said that you can get anything there from anti-tank missiles and anti-aircraft guns to replica Purdey and Holland & Holland shotguns.'

'So it's a no-brainer then,' Jimbo said. 'Why eat hamburger when you can eat steak?'

'But why eat either if there's a deep-fried Mars Bar on offer, eh Jock?' Geordie said, ducking under the retaliatory swipe from Jock.

They commandeered the battered pick-up truck that the Scaleybacks had been using and drove south out of town. Darra Adam Khel turned out to be a straggling village of wood and mud brick buildings in a narrow valley between the towering ranges of hills. As they approached, it looked no different from any of the half dozen other villages they'd driven through on the way there, but as they reached the outskirts, they heard gunfire. Shepherd shot a quizzical glance at Jock. 'It's probably nothing,' Jock said.

'Apparently it's like an Arab wedding every day of the week here, because they test their weapons by firing them up in the air.'

'They've not heard of the laws of gravity then?' Geordie said. 'What goes up, must come down, and all that? It must be like a monsoon of rounds at times.'

'None of them can shoot straight,' Jimbo said, 'so wherever all those rounds do come down, it won't be on their own heads.'

'Then let's hope it's not on ours instead,' said Geordie.

The main road through the Darra Adam Khel bazaar was lined with stalls. The streets were packed with men, most dressed in the shalwar kameez, some also wearing traditional Afghan pakol or karakul hats. There were a few women to be seen as well, but only a few, dressed in blue, mauve and green burqas. When they saw Shepherd and his mates approaching, all of them stopped and turned their faces to the wall until the foreigners had passed them by.

Some of the stalls sold food, clothing, sandals cut from recycled car tyres, empty bottles and jars, and the pots, pans, shovels, buckets and scythes that the local metal workers made from shell casings and other scrap. There were small boys, selling single cigarettes from packets that still had the American PX markings on them and, flanked by heavy-set body-guards, money changers who sat cross-legged with thick bundles of well-worn rupees, Afghanis, dollars, dirhams, Saudi riyals and pounds sterling laid out on scraps of cardboard in front of them. However, unlike most of the village bazaars that the SAS men had seen, the vast majority of stalls were filled with weapons and munitions and most of their attention was focussed on them.

Between each stall, at right angles to the street, there were arcades lined with tiny workshops. Columns of oily black smoke spiralled upwards from small forges where little boys dripped sweat as they worked the leather bellows forcing air through the glowing coals. The air was full of the clamour of metal on metal, with gunsmiths, some of them also just boys, squatting cross-legged in the dust, turning out weapons using nothing but hand-tools and small drill-presses powered by banks of Honda generators that added another layer of noise to the general din, and yet more smoke to the pall from the diesel trucks rumbling through on their way to and from Peshawar.

Shepherd and his team stopped to watch the craftsman as they fashioned beautifully-made weapons using only the most primitive tools. The goods they sold ranged from pistols, rifles and semi-automatics, right up to rocket-propelled grenade launchers, mortars and even small artillery pieces. Jimbo picked up a weapon from one stall and turned it over in his hands. 'Unbelievable,' he said. 'It's a fake but you'd struggle to know it. Look, they've even copied the serial number from the original.'

Jock nodded. 'I've heard it said that you can show them any weapon from anywhere in the world and they'll knock off a replica for you inside a week and only an expert would be able to tell it apart from the real thing.'

'We should bring them a Cruise missile then,' Geordie said, 'and really test that theory.'

'Do you know what they call guns here?' Jock said, ignoring the interruption. 'They call them "The ornaments of the Pushtuns". They don't go in for jewels or china figurines on the mantelpiece, just AK-47s and RPGs.'

'And do you know what else?' Jimbo said, holding up a Kalashnikov, 'Look at the price, it's unbelievable! You can buy a rifle for the same price as a half-kilo bag of sugar.'

Shepherd and the others spent an eye-opening couple of hours wandering through the souq. The smell of animal dung mingled with the smoke hanging in the air, and the gutters were choked with refuse and raw sewage, around which clouds of flies buzzed. An ice-seller's cart full of blocks of ice carved from the frozen lakes and glaciers of the mountains was covered in filthy sacking to protect it from the heat. Next to him, incongruously, a street vendor had set up a stall where he was cooking naan breads on a hand-beaten metal dome propped over a blazing fire that was accelerating the melting of his neighbour's ice.

Many of the weapons on sale at the other stalls had been made in the souq, but most of the rest looked to be of Soviet origin. 'There must be more ex-Sov kit here than there is in Russia,' Jimbo said, shaking his head in disbelief.

'Yeah, a hell of a lot of it was captured from Soviet troops during the Russian Vietnam, when they got sent packing from Afghanistan with their tails between their legs.'

'There's plenty of other stuff too, though,' Shepherd said, 'including a few bits of the latest Brit and Yank weaponry.'

'And it will have come from the same source,' Jock said, 'either stolen or sold by some of our beloved Afghan allies that we and the Yanks have been training.'

'It's not all modern kit though,' Jimbo said, holding up a bolt-action Lee-Enfield rifle that might even have been a left-over from the British Afghan Wars in the nineteenth century.

After working their way from one end of the souq to the other, they eventually approached an elderly dealer with a stall full of semi-automatic rifles. Shepherd looked over a few weapons before deciding on an aged AK 47.

'Blimey, that looks like it's seen a serious amount of action,' Jimbo said as Shepherd examined it. 'Are you sure it'll still fire?'

'Let's find out, shall we?' Shepherd said. The blue-ing on the gun had been worn away, exposing the bare metal underneath, but it still looked mechanically perfect. Shepherd stripped it down and reassembled it, then took it outside the stall and test-fired it, aiming at a scrap of yellowing paper caught on a thorn bush on the scrubby hillside behind the bazaar. The first round kicked up a puff of dust from a bare patch of earth just to the right of the bush. He adjusted the sight, but slightly over-compensated and this time missed by a couple of inches to the left of his target. He made a further adjustment and fired again, and this time the piece of paper disintegrated as the round struck home.

He nodded in satisfaction, added a stack of boxes of rounds and, after haggling half-heartedly over the price for a few moments, he handed the dealer a wad of dollars.

'So you're into buying antiques now?' Jimbo said, still eyeing the weapon with suspicion.

'Listen smart-arse, it will be dependable and it won't let me down,' said Shepherd. 'It fires a standard round, no one is going to be able to claim that it's of UK origin if it falls into the wrong hands, and even better, nobody is going to want to try to knock me off to get their hands on it, which they might be tempted to do if I got myself a brand new weapon instead.'

Jimbo thought about it for a moment then shrugged and said 'You know what Spider? You're not quite as dumb as you look.' He bought a similar weapon for himself, closely followed by Geordie and Jock.

While they were buying the weapons, Shepherd was very aware of the small crowd of men clustered around the stall, watching them. It might just have been the natural curiosity of villagers not used to seeing strangers in their souq, except that he saw two of them muttering to each other. They had black, kohl-rimmed eyes and were dressed in the garb of the Taliban's 'soldier monks' with their black turbans folded into an elaborate cockscomb shape and a long forked tail of the cloth hanging down their backs. They directed malevolent stares at the SAS men before slipping away down an alley between the stalls.

As he looked round, Shepherd caught Jock's eye. 'I can remember in Belfast when you'd see people doing that,' Jock said. 'And five minutes later there'd be a posse of Paddies appearing in masks and black berets, waving Armalites. I'm getting much the same feeling now.'

'Me too,' Shepherd said, 'so let's not hang around long enough to find out if you're right. We don't want to get into a shoot-out here before we've even begun the op.'

Taking their newly-acquired weapons with them, they moved off at an apparently unhurried pace, but one that covered the ground quickly. They slipped easily into the familiar patrol discipline so that even walking down a crowded street, Shepherd was acting as lead scout in front, Jock was tail-end Charlie watching the rear, and the other two kept alert for threats from either flank.

Jimbo was the first to spot trouble. 'There's a group of four blokes keeping pace with us on the parallel street to the left,' he said. 'They're waiting at each cross-street to make sure we're still heading in the same direction, and then moving ahead again.'

'I've got company too,' Geordie said. 'Four blokes, doing the same thing on the other side.'

'And I've got another two on our tail,' Jock said.

'Nothing visible ahead as yet, so that's ten altogether,' Shepherd said. 'Plus whatever might be waiting further up the street.'

'Ten against four hardly seems fair, does it?' Geordie said with a broad grin. 'Shall we wait for the rest to get here and make it more of a fair fight?'

'Nah, you can get too much of a good thing,' Shepherd said, 'let's get to it right now. Okay, at the next cross-street, we turn left and go like hell.'

The SAS men sauntered to the next street, for all the world like a group of friends out for an afternoon stroll, but as they approached the corner, Shepherd said, 'On my count: Three... Two... One... Go!' They swung left, sprinted the length of the cross-street and arrived in the midst of the four men who had been trailing them on that side with the force of a bomb. Shepherd hit the lead man, one of the Taliban soldier monks, with the butt of his rifle and heard the sound of splintering bone as his nose disintegrated under the impact of the blow.

As his victim crumpled to the ground, blood spurting from his smashed nose, Shepherd drove an elbow into the windpipe of the next man who was fumbling at his belt, trying to pull a knife from his waistband. Geordie followed up with a vicious kick to the man's balls and he collapsed in a heap, emitting piercing, high-pitched screams, while his knife fell from his limp fingers and skittered away into the refuse-strewn gutter. Jimbo felled the third assailant with a fusillade of savage punches and karate chops and Jock dropped the fourth, Glaswegian bar brawl style, head-butting him and then kneeing him in the balls for good measure as he fell.

At a warning shout from Geordie, the four SAS men swivelled to face the remainder of the pack of assailants who, surprised by the sudden change of direction, were only now catching up with their targets. Four more men went down before the SAS team's relentless onslaught. Whatever fighting skills the attackers had learned on the streets of Peshawar or Kabul were no match for the cold, brutal ferocity of the SAS men. Shepherd and his mates had been schooled in countless hours of training and unarmed combat. That included "milling", where no attempt to defend yourself was permitted and all you could do was try to land more punches on your opponent than he could land on you. There were also training assignments where SAS men were deliberately sent unarmed into the most rough and dangerous gangland areas of Britain, where every stranger was treated as an enemy. Going into pubs that were thieves' kitchens for criminals and drug dealers, the only order was 'Remain there for an hour and if compromised, fight your way out.' Any who failed to do so successfully were thrown out of the Regiment and RTU'd – sent back to their former unit.

Given those levels of street-fighting skills, there was only ever going to be one winner. Only two of the attackers were now still standing. One of them, the other Taliban soldier monk, unslung his rifle from his shoulder and, after fumbling with the safety catch, swung up the barrel to bring it to bear on the SAS men, but even as he did Shepherd was already launching himself into a dive. His shoulder hit the attacker's chest in a murderous crash tackle, sending him sprawling on his back as the air whistled from his lungs. Shepherd followed up with savage, chopping blows to the man's nose and Adam's apple, leaving him in a crumpled, comatose heap.

The last of the ten men, desperate to avoid the fate of his companions, had already turned on his heel and begun to flee back the way he'd come, swerving through the crowds of curious onlookers who had stopped to watch the brawl. Catching sight of the baleful stares from the SAS men, the spectators suddenly remembered pressing business elsewhere and hurried away.

'Well, that was a nice little work-out,' Jimbo said, brushing the dust from his jacket. 'Good thing you bought that AK, Spider, though it's a bit of a shame about the bloodstains on the butt.'

'Those guys trailing us were a bit of a worry though,' Shepherd said. 'I definitely got the impression that they were more than just a bunch of muggers looking to grab some tourists' wallets. They knew what they were doing.'

'Yeah, for once you're not talking your normal shite, Spider,' Jock said, 'so I tell you what, let's not hang around to find out if there are any more locals out there who want to try their luck with us.'

Still keeping a wary eye out for potential trouble, they walked to the end of the street, then jumped into their battered pick-up and joined the slow-moving queue of traffic heading back to Peshawar.

'Where the hell are all these people going?' Geordie said. 'The traffic's worse than the Tyne Tunnel on a Friday afternoon.'

The others exchanged smiles. Wherever they were in the world, Geordie was legendary for his ability to find something that reminded him of Newcastle.

'Yeah,' Jimbo said, 'except the traffic in the Tyne Tunnel isn't carrying opium or weapons.'

'I wouldn't bet on it,' Geordie said.

They reached the safe house without any further incident. Ahmad had obviously been pacing up and down the garden, wearing a furrow in the grass as he waited for them to return, and he greeted them with relief. 'I've been cursing myself for letting you go to the souq without escorting you there,' he said. 'I was worried you might be attacked.'

'You were right to be worried, because we were attacked,' Jock said with a broad smile. 'But I can guarantee that it will be the last attack they'll be staging for quite some time.'

That evening they made sure their kit was packed and ready for an early start the next morning but, with the inevitable exception of Jock who, as usual, slept like a baby, the rest of them slept fitfully through the night, anxiously waiting for the dawn. Before they set off, Jock called them together. 'It probably goes without saying, but I've seen a lot more of this country and the guys we might be fighting with and against than you, so I just wanted to stress that if I'm wounded and you have to leave me behind, I want a bullet between the eyes before you do so.' He paused, fixing each of them with his gaze. 'And I'd advise you all to make the same request because this is not a country where you want to be taken prisoner. All of them, even guys like Ahmad, would cut off your balls, disembowel you or flay the skin from your back, without even blinking.'

Shepherd glanced around the others. 'I think we'd all say the same,' he said. 'Let's just hope it doesn't come to that.'

Chapter 5

Shepherd and his patrol left the safe house before first light, led by Ahmad and his men. Geordie had covered his thinning hair with a pakol – the soft, round and very warm Afghan hat – and at a distance, dressed in Afghan clothes, they would all have passed for natives. But while most of them were sufficiently sun- and wind-burned to look like an Afghan to a casual glance, Jock's Glaswegian pallor never altered. Sun and wind only made his face red and as soon as he was out of the sun, his face resumed its normal pale skin tone. He could not have been a more obvious Brit if he'd wrapped a union jack round his head and even smothered in fake tan, he still stood out as a foreigner.

Just as they were leaving the grounds, Geordie excused himself and ran back into the building. He returned a couple of minutes later. 'What was that about?' Shepherd said. 'Did you forget your make-up bag or your travel sickness pills or something?'

'Very funny,' Geordie said. 'Actually, I went back to tell the Scaleybacks to get their kit together and move to the High Commission because we think it is too dangerous for them to stay here.'

'Sound advice,' said Shepherd.

'You'd think so, right? But do you know what? They told me to mind my own business, so fuck 'em.'

'Well, you tried,' Jock said, 'so if things do go tits up, at least you'll have a clear conscience.'

A lorry, garlanded with plastic flowers and with the flags of Pakistan and Afghanistan flying from its roof, was waiting at the corner of the street. The destination board above the windscreen read "Kabul". They all clambered aboard, squeezing in among a dozen other men in tribal costume and a few minutes later, the lorry lumbered out into the traffic. It turned onto the road to the west, and a few miles further on, as the road bore round to the north, they passed through the stone gateway marking the start of the legendary and notorious Khyber Pass. A Victorian folly, modelled on a Norman castle, the gateway's twin stone towers were capped by battlements and Shepherd could see the barrels of a pair of antique cannons poking out above them.

'Brits have been fighting tribesmen here since Queen Victoria was a lass,' Jock said, still revelling in his self-appointed role as their local guide and expert.

Geordie shrugged. 'Pity they never got round to updating the artillery, then.'

'There are no British soldiers here now,' Ahmad said. 'The lower reaches of the Pass are controlled by

Levies of the Pakistani army. They collect the taxes demanded by the authorities in Islamabad but they also make sure to extort an extra tribute from every traveller for themselves as well.'

Shepherd smiled. 'Why do I sense a "but" coming?'

Ahmad grinned, glanced around him and then dropped his voice. 'But of course we'll be paying no taxes because I know a short cut?'

As the lorry laboured up the pass, twisting and turning around the bends, the mountains rose steadily higher on either side and the valley walls pressed closer around them. The edge of the road dropped away almost sheer in places and the rusting wreckage of lorries lost in winter storms, accidents, ambushes or avalanches could be glimpsed here and there among the rocks and the coarse, thorny scrub that cloaked the lower hillsides. Above them there was nothing but bare earth, rock and scree, with vultures and ravens circling in the sky, riding the thermals rising up the mountain faces.

They passed through Kandi Kotal, the last settlement of any size before the border town of Torkham. A little further on, still a couple of kilometres short of the border, when the lorry was grinding up the steepest gradient on its way to the summit and barely making five miles an hour, Ahmad gathered the bundle that held his belongings and gave the nod to his comrades and the SAS men. He stepped to the back of the truck and jumped down into the road. Their fellow-passengers watched without obvious curiosity or interest as Shepherd's patrol and the rest of the mujahideen followed suit taking their equipment and weapons with them.

The lorry rumbled on, grinding its slow way towards the top of the pass, while the SAS men left the road at once with Ahmad and his mujahideen leading the way. They struck off up the mountain on a path so faint it was nothing more than a thin wavering line of slightly paler grey against the dark rock of the barren hillside. They climbed steadily, higher and higher into the mountain range. The summits closest to them, high though they were, proved to be mere foothills, for beyond them they caught glimpses of rank upon rank of towering saw-toothed peaks, thrown into even sharper relief by the low sunlight, with their summits permanently clad in snow.

At first they were clambering through boulder fields and scrambling up screes and hillsides of bare rock, but they soon reached the snow-line where the going underfoot became even more difficult. They crossed patches of coarse, gritty snow that must have lain there for months, melting a little in the sun's rays by day and then re-freezing as the temperatures plummeted in the brutal cold in the depths of the Afghan winter nights. In other parts of the mountain there were fields of freshly fallen powder snow, so soft and yielding that it would bear no weight and the heavy-laden men floundered their way through it, their boots struggling for purchase in snow as fine and formless as flour.

Above the snow-fields there were ice-crusted crags, where the track, such as it was, wove its way through narrow clefts in the rock and they had to fight for every handhold as they clawed their way upwards with hands that were numbed and clumsy from cold. The winds knifed through even the warmest clothes and stung their cheeks with shards of ice, and even out of the wind, the cold bit like a dog. When Shepherd raised his canteen to his lips to drink, not a drop emerged because the water in it had frozen solid. Where the path sloped less steeply, any patches of ground scoured clear of snow by the relentless winds were often covered in sheet ice.

As they climbed, their eyes were constantly flickering to the masses of new snow clinging to the slopes, peaks and ridges above them, threatening an avalanche that might sweep them to their deaths. Although the sun made the air temperature a little warmer as it rose higher in the sky, its effects made the going underfoot even more treacherous, overlaying the ice with a thin film of meltwater that made the surface still more slick and slippery. It was exhausting work and, supremely fit as the SAS men were, they were soon gasping and panting under the weight of their packs in the thin air. Shepherd could hear his breath rasping and the blood pounding in his ears as he plodded on up the mountain side.

Although they were equally burdened, their escorts appeared to skip along, barely seeming to notice the snow and the steep gradients, but then they were happy because they were going home.

'Know what?' Jimbo said, shaking his head in disbelief. 'These guys would absolutely walk Selection. They'd be up and down Pen-y-fan twice or three times in the time it would take us to get over it once.'

'True,' Shepherd said. 'But if all there was to Special Forces soldiering was climbing mountains, Sherpa Tensing and his mates would have put us all out of a job years ago.'

Their lack of acclimatisation at altitude and the relentless pace their escorts were setting was already beginning to tell on Jimbo. He was struggling to keep up with the others, his breathing sounded harsh and laboured, and he was coughing frequently. Shepherd nudged Geordie, the patrol medic, and murmured 'Looks like Jimbo's really struggling for breath.'

'I know,' Geordie said. 'I've already been keeping an eye on him. It looks like altitude sickness and we haven't got any oxygen so if he gets any worse the only cure will be to get him down to a lower altitude.'

'And that's not happening,' Jimbo said, having struggled up to them and caught the tail-end of the conversation. 'I'm fine, just give me a moment and then we'll move on.'

'You don't look fine,' Geordie said.

Jimbo shrugged. 'To misquote Churchill: And you're ugly, but in the morning I'll be better.'

'Apart from the breathlessness and the cough, what are your other symptoms?' asked Geordie.

'A bit of a headache and nausea, that's all. Nothing I can't handle,' he said as he saw Geordie's sceptical look.

During one of their increasingly frequent rest stops to allow Jimbo to catch his breath, Ahmad beckoned to Shepherd and pointed down, far below them, at the queue of traffic at the border checkpoint. Using his binoculars, Shepherd saw the row of concrete blocks funnelling the traffic into a single file as it approached the huddle of buildings at the border. Street vendors had set up stalls at either side of the road, selling food, water and tea to the drivers waiting their turn to cross.

The gaudy lorry that they had recently left had now reached the checkpoint, where it had been stopped by the Pakistani troops. Through his binoculars, Shepherd could see that it had been pulled over to one side of the road and everything on board was being unloaded from it and closely examined. Its passengers were standing huddled together, while a Pakistani officer paced around them, pulling each one out in turn for questioning.

'They seem to be looking for something,' Shepherd said with a smile.

'Yes,' Ahmad said. 'Us.'

They moved on and as they climbed higher still, the Kabul road came into full view as it began to trace its route across the high Afghan plain towards the capital.

So clear was the air at this altitude that from miles away they could pick out small details: houses, vehicles, groups of people trekking through the foot-hills. To either side of the road, littering the snow- and ice-filled gullies, they could also see the rusting skeletons of vehicles that, for whatever reason, hadn't made it over the pass. Stripped of body parts, engines, tyres and everything removable – as in any Third World country, nothing was ever wasted in Afghanistan – the remaining frames had been left lit-tering the slopes and ravines like the skeletons of the dead animals picked clean by vultures and ravens.

'It's like the aftermath of a demolition derby down there,' Geordie said. 'They do have a lot of acci-dents, don't they?'

'They do,' Jock said, 'but I suspect that most of those wrecks would be military vehicles ambushed by the mujahideen during the Soviet war.'

It was easy to spot the lorry they had vacated mak-ing its slow progress out of the mountains and on to the plain. Suddenly, like watching a silent movie, they saw a series of explosions engulf the vehicle. They were too far away to hear any noise but as the truck disappeared behind a wall of flame and a cloud of oily black smoke, it was obvious that it had been ambushed.

'Well, the Soviets may have gone, but the ambushes obviously haven't,' Geordie said. 'Bloody good job we decided to walk. There's a lot to be said for Shanks's pony.'

Shepherd nodded. 'It looks like someone really is out to stop us. The question is, why?'

'I'm not sure these guys ever need a reason to start a war,' Jock said, 'but you've got a point. There are plenty of Western military teams here training up the locals, so why are they focusing on us?'

'Maybe they aren't,' Jimbo said. 'Maybe we're just being paranoid.'

'No, it's more than paranoia,' Shepherd said. 'The bastards really are out to get us.'

Now on high alert, Ahmad deployed his fighters as a screen around the Special Forces patrol. He had his men in front and on all sides and at the rear of Shepherd and his men. When they approached any location that might be a source of danger, the Brits were made to take cover while the mujahideen went ahead to check out the area.

After a while this began to grate on Jock's nerves. 'Does he think we're scared or something?' he said. 'We're not little old ladies, we're the SAS for fuck's sake.'

'Yeah,' Jimbo said. 'We can't sit here twiddling our thumbs while they are out there taking all the risks.'

'Don't worry about it,' Shepherd said. 'It's just part of the culture. We're their guests, so they're looking after us and they've got a good reason for doing it well because if something does happen to us, their honour means they'll have to avenge it.'

'So is that the reason there are so many life-long blood feuds here?'

'Yeah, it's just like the Hatfields and McCoys,' Shepherd said, 'only with heavy weapons.'

Geordie looked blank. 'The who?'

'It's a famous Appalachian mountain feud.'

'Appalachi-what?'

'Appalachia,' said Shepherd. 'It's a region in the Eastern United States, from the south of New York to northern Alabama, Mississippi and Georgia.'

Geordie gave a slow shake of his head. 'If there's ever an SAS pub quiz team, Spider, you'll be a shoe-in for captain. Where do you learn all this shit?'

'I read a few books, Geordie. You know, bundles of paper with writing on them?'

'Yeah, I know,' said Geordie, grinning. 'They're dead handy if you run out of bog paper.'

Although they could see for miles in the thin, clear air, the downside was that also meant they were visible from far away themselves. Once they had gone far enough from the road to avoid immediate danger, they rested up for the rest of the daylight hours, trying to grab what sleep they could despite the bitter cold by sheltering in a shallow dip between two boulders and huddling together for warmth.

Late that afternoon, Shepherd watched the line of the sunset inching up the wall of the mountains until only the snow capped peaks were still bathed in a red glow, and then woke his comrades. They ate some of their rations and then moved off at once. The SAS men used their passive night goggles to see their way, though their Afghan guides were equally sure-footed with nothing more than the moon and the stars to light their way. They walked all night and just before dawn they found a dry-stone goat-pen in a hanging valley. They sheltered there the following day, sharing the space with a long-dead goat that had been mummified by the dry, cold winds, so that patches of fur and skin as hard and tough as leather still clung to its bones. 'Facially he reminds me of the CO,' was Jock's only comment, as he settled down next to it and, as usual, was asleep in seconds.

On the next day, they rested through the daylight hours in an abandoned and partly collapsed hut, used by shepherds bringing their flocks up to the high pastures in summer. It overlooked a half-frozen lake, with water that was the colour of agate but so clear that, even though it was several metres deep, Shepherd could see shoals of small fish were swimming close to the bottom.

Jimbo seemed to have recovered from his altitude sickness and even though they were moving through the high mountains, often with little more than goat-tracks to follow, the SAS men and their guides were covering the ground at a relentless pace, taking advantage of the long late-winter nights to walk for up to fourteen hours.

By the end of the third night they were already descending from the mountains on to the plain around Kabul. As they dropped below the tree-line, they found some shelter, first among isolated larch and rowan trees, their branches twisted and contorted by the relentless winds, while lower on the slopes there were dense stands of cedars that filled the air with the rich scent of cedarwood. They had now entered more populated areas and they passed through numerous fields of opium poppies that had been milked of their sap the previous autumn but still had seed heads so withered and dried by sun, wind and frost that they rattled like tiny maracas as the SAS men brushed against them.

Even though they were still moving only at night, the SAS team and their mujahideen minders found that their problems were increasing. No matter how carefully and quietly they moved, wherever they went they were accompanied by the constant barking of dogs. Usually the wild dogs prowling the outskirts of the towns and villages, or sniffing around the isolated buildings between them, would pick up their scent or the slight sounds that they made and would start howling. The noise then alerted the many domestic dogs in the nearby villages and they in turn took up the chorus of barking and howling, alerting their owners in turn, who would then have to be avoided or pacified.

On one occasion, the villagers alerted the local warlord and Ahmad's mujahideen and the SAS men found their way blocked by a hastily-improvised checkpoint manned by thirty or forty heavily armed tribesmen. If it had come to a shoot-out, even with their second-hand weapons Shepherd was confident that they could have dealt with the threat, but he did not want to be fighting a running battle all the way across Afghanistan. He took Ahmad to one side and after a short discussion he produced a bribe from the roll of dollars that he was carrying for exactly that purpose. After a token show of reluctance it was enough to persuade the warlord to allow them to pass unhindered. In return they were issued with a piece of grubby paper covered in inscriptions from the Koran and with the greasy thumbprint of the warlord added to it as his official seal of approval.

'How far will that get us, Ahmad?' Shepherd said, as they moved on, keeping a wary eye behind them in case the warlord was tempted to find out how many more dollars the SAS men were carrying.

Ahmad shrugged. 'As far as the next warlord's territory and no further,' he said. 'Perhaps ten kilometres, no more than that. They are each a law unto themselves.'

The mujahideen still maintained their screen around Shepherd and his patrol, but now at a much greater distance. They fanned out to watch for more pickets, sentries or armed patrols from whatever factions controlled the territory they were crossing. The eyesight of the mujahideen was phenomenal, far better than Shepherd's even when he was using his passive night goggles, but the lack of radios hampered communications and inevitably that slowed the rate of march.

The landscape was also working against them. There were also dozens of swiftly flowing rivers and streams dissecting the area. All the rivers they encountered were swollen with meltwater and were higher, colder and faster-flowing than any of the group were happy with. By trial and error they discovered that the most efficient method was to cross each river linked together by ropes in threes without their equipment, and then bring their kit across afterwards, using their ropes to haul it over. Despite this, even the smallest river crossing proved to be cold, laborious and very time consuming, sapping their strength and resources.

Bridges had been constructed across some of the rivers in their path, but that was often a mixed blessing. The first sight of one bridge, spanning a ferocious torrent that was rumbling and racing between the glistening walls of the chasm beneath it, caused all the SAS men to catch their breath. It was a frail-looking structure made of thick, rough-cut planks of wood cantilevered out from the banks, with just a narrow, curving plank measuring no more than six inches in width – a pine tree that and been split lengthwise – forming the centre span. There was no handrail, not even a rope and the plank, saturated by the spray from the torrent, looked as slippery as a wet seal. However, the only alternative to using the bridge was to make a detour to a point much nearer to the source of the torrent higher in the mountains adding at least day to their journey, or descend towards the plains, where they were much more likely to be detected and intercepted by enemy troops. Shepherd steeled himself to lead the way across, though he was far from happy about the prospect.

The fast-rushing waters of the river below the bridge were a beautiful milky jade colour as the light reflected from millions of mica flakes ground out of the mountains by the glaciers and suspended in the water, but Shepherd had no time to admire its beauty as he began to inch his way out across the narrow span. The old timbers creaked ominously as he moved towards the centre, and the plank at the middle was so slimy and slippery that he was forced to drop to his hands and knees and crawl across it. As he did so, he was just shifting one hand a little further along the plank when his knee slipped and skidded off the edge of it. He lurched to that side and for a moment was teetering over the drop to the foaming water below, held there only by the grip of his other hand. He managed to hold on, the veins in his neck standing out from the effort as he clamped his other hand back on the plank, dragged himself upright again and regained his balance, though it was some seconds before he could slow the wild beating of his heart.

'Come on, Spider, stop pissing around!' shouted Geordie from behind him. 'We don't have time to play games.'

Spider grinned, regained his composure and moved on and a few seconds later, he was safe on the other side. Undaunted by his own close call, he even managed to indulge in the traditional banter and barracking as the other three made their own tentative journeys across.

'Come on Jimbo, we are the pilgrims, remember,' he said, as Jimbo reached the slippery plank at the centre of the bridge and began inching his way across it. 'We feel no fear.'

'Yeah, you certainly looked like you weren't bricking it at all when you were clinging to the plank like a lifebelt in a stormy sea,' Jimbo said.

When all four SAS men were safely across, they watched Ahmad and his men cross. All of them did so standing upright and all were as sure-footed as mountain goats, crossing as if they were strolling in a suburban park, not walking along a narrow, slippery plank from which they could easily have fallen to their deaths.

'That's what I call a failure of imagination,' Jock said.

Shepherd gave a rueful smile. 'I could certainly have done with one of those when I was going across.'

'Is gainly the opposite of ungainly?' asked Jimbo. 'Because those guys are gainly.' He nodded at Spider. 'You, not so much.'

Each morning during the march, while the others used the daylight hours to rest, Ahmad would disappear and sniff around the local villages for whatever bits of intelligence he could glean. It was potentially dangerous because, although the Afghan tradition of hospitality to visitors might once have made strangers welcome, the decades of war and factional fighting now made every visitor a potential object of suspicion and hostility. What Ahmad did learn from those few villagers who were willing to talk to him made disturbing news for the SAS men. 'The whole area has been put on a state of high alert,' he said when he returned from his latest intelligence gathering mission. 'The villagers have been told to watch out for any sign of a group of British soldiers who are said to be trying to infiltrate into the Panjshir Valley.' He paused, checking the SAS men's expressions. 'And in case any of you are wondering, let me promise you something: wherever the leak came from, it did not come from me or my men. They know that I would cut out the tongue of any man who betrayed our secrets.'

'We believe you, Ahmad,' Shepherd said, 'but there's clearly been a leak somewhere along the line and that's only going to make our task more difficult. What else did you hear?'

'That the villagers I spoke to have heard that a large reward is being offered for information on the British soldiers' whereabouts, or for the soldiers themselves, dead or alive. But they didn't seem to have heard anything more tangible than that. Just the rumours that always swirl around these regions like the dust devils stirred from the soil by the summer winds.' He grinned, clearly pleased at his elegant use of language. Shepherd could see Jock about to make a cutting remark so he silenced him with a glare.

Even more disturbing than this intelligence was the news that one of Ahmad's men brought about the largest river that they would have to cross before they could reach the Panjshir. With the river levels so high, they had been planning to use the only bridge in the area, but Ahmad's man had heard talk from the local villagers that a force of troops equipped with a tank and heavy weapons had been deployed on the far bank of the river to cover the crossing point.

'This is a major problem for us, Spider,' Ahmad said, his brow furrowed. 'If we are not able to cross using the bridge, the river is not fordable for many days march in either direction. So somehow we have got to find a way across.'

Shepherd nodded. 'Just keep us heading for the bridge, Ahmad, and we'll find a way over the river at some point, even if we have to fight our way across.'

They approached the bridge under the cover of darkness the following night. Using their passive night goggles, the SAS men could see that there was indeed a body of troops of about platoon strength, dug in on the far side of the river. They used the cover of some thorny scrub to set up an observation post from which they could keep watch and then spent the remainder of the night and the whole of the next day OP'ing the bridge and its defenders.

The bridge itself was a flimsy-looking affair, a suspension bridge made of rope and rough planks, and barely wide enough to take a loaded donkey-cart. A tracked BMP armoured personnel carrier had been drawn up on the far bank, at an oblique angle to the bridge and within a few feet of it. Anyone approaching the bridge from the side where Ahmad and the SAS men were in hiding would have to run the gauntlet of the armoured personnel carrier's 76 mm gun pointing across the river at the entrance to the bridge and the AT-4 Spigot anti-tank rocket mounted above the gun. To complete the picture, the guards had also set up a 12.7 heavy machine gun on top of the small turret.

The bridge itself looked too fragile to take the weight of a horse and cart, let alone an armoured military vehicle, but while that would prevent the enemy from using the vehicle to cross the river and attack them, its armament would make a frontal assault over the bridge by the SAS men and their mujahideen allies a suicide mission. Just to increase their concerns still further, in all the time that they kept the armoured personnel carrier under observation, the machine gun was never left unattended, even for an instant, but was manned continuously by one of the sentries. A full-frontal assault would be nothing less than suicide.

CHAPTER 6

After last light Shepherd called together his comrades and held a quick Chinese Parliament.
Everyone, including Ahmad, was encouraged to par-
ticipate and put forward any ideas that they had for
avoiding or destroying the obstacle in their path.
'My mates don't need reminding of this, Ahmad,'
Shepherd said, 'but for your benefit, we have an old
adage in the SAS: if you don't contribute to the plan
or raise any objections to it when it's being discussed
and formulated, you don't have the right to criticise
it afterwards, even if it all turns to rat-shit. Okay?' He
waited for an answering nod before continuing.

After a few minutes' of the usual heated discussion, with no quarter asked or given, Shepherd
was happy that they had the basis of a plan which,
although high risk, had a reasonable chance of success. He quickly outlined the tasks that the various
individuals would be expected to carry out as part of
the plan and as usual with a patrol full of spiky and
opinionated, but hugely skilful members, the alloca-
tion of tasks led to more dissension and argument.

However as patrol leader Shepherd eventually cut the wrangling short and asserted his authority.

Offended by the minor role that his mujahideen had been given in the plan, Ahmad took the most convincing. Ahmad was all for charging across the bridge with guns blazing. 'The aim is not to start a firefight with them, Ahmad,' Shepherd said, 'or at least, if we do, it can only be on our terms, not theirs. This is to be a precision operation and it depends on the bravery and skill of trained Special Forces soldiers, the guys in my patrol in other words.'

Ahmad bristled. 'You doubt my men's bravery?

'Of course not,' said Shepherd, putting a hand on the man's shoulder. 'Only a fool doubts the courage of Afghan fighters, but we have to fight smart. Your men are brave, no question of that, but they don't have the skill sets yet. I promise you, they will have by the time we've finished training them after we reach the Panjshir Valley. But as things stand right now, if this attack is going to succeed it will depend on precisely calculated and calibrated lines of fire and only my men have the training and experience to do that.'

Having at last convinced Ahmad of the wisdom of the plan, Shepherd sent him to deploy his men as a defensive screen behind them while he and the other three spent several hours carrying out line of sight and firing position tests. It was a time-consuming and dangerous exercise, because the sentry on the armoured personnel carrier was looking in their direction. The SAS men used every scrap of cover to conceal their movements as they advanced from one position to another, and threaded grasses, leaves and stems from the vegetation growing around the river bank into their clothes to camouflage themselves and break up their outlines, ensured that they were not compromised. They were helped by the fact that the sentry was less-than focussed on his task and was often talking to his colleagues and smoking cigarettes with them.

Eventually everybody was happy with their firing positions, lines of sight and their roles in the attack. Shepherd and Ahmad then began their part of the plan by setting off to run downstream along the river bank carrying only their weapons, a couple of hand grenades each, and the "lowering lines" that Shepherd had collected from the other members of his patrol. These were the twenty foot long, braided nylon cord ropes that were usually used, dangling below them, to hold their containers of weapons and equipment when they were parachuting. However, they had proved so useful in combat situations that most Special Forces soldiers carried lowering lines on ops as a matter of course, even when no parachuting was going to be involved. Although they would stretch when wet, they were impossible to break.

Shepherd and Ahmad ranged far downstream along the river bank, continually scanning the surface of the water and the near and opposite banks, looking for the least dangerous crossing place they could find. After several miles of fierce, rock-strewn rapids and a current so strong that even the most powerful swimmer would have been swept away, the river broadened slightly and the water slowed a little, flowing a little less ferociously around a shallow bend.

'This looks to be about as good as we are going to get,' Shepherd said. 'Okay, strip off and let's get going.'

Ahmad did a double-take. 'It is not normal for a Muslim to be naked in front of a stranger, Spider.'

'I know that, but these are hardly normal circumstances and after living in each other's pockets for the last couple of weeks, we're hardly strangers either,' said Shepherd.

Ahmad didn't look convinced.

'I promise not to peek,' said Shepherd. 'So let's get to it.'

Ahmad hesitated a moment longer, but then quickly stripped to his underclothes, before looking to Shepherd for further instructions. He packed their clothes and weapons into a plastic rubble sack from his bergen, sealed it with a knot and tied it onto the lowering rope and then, roping themselves together, they stepped gingerly into the raging torrent. The shock of the cold made them both gasp for breath and the force of the water was so strong that almost immediately, Ahmad was swept off his feet. As the rope snapped taut, he nearly dragged Shepherd under as well. However, bracing himself both against the current and the pull of Ahmad, who was unable to swim and floundering helplessly out of his depth, gasping for breath, Shepherd managed to get back to the bank and then reeled Ahmad back in like a stranded fish.

Ahmad lay on the riverbank for a few minutes, gasping and coughing up water, before he was ready to carry on. 'Okay,' Shepherd said with a wry smile. 'That didn't work too well, did it? So if you've recovered enough to give it another try, let's see if we can make the crossing a different way.'

'I'm not a great swimmer,' said Ahmad.

'I picked up on that,' said Shepherd with a rueful smile.

He tied one end of the lowering lines around his own waist and while Ahmad took the strain on the bank, Shepherd eased himself out into the current. This time, instead of trying to wade across, he dived under the surface and swimming as hard as physically possible, he swung like a pendulum on the end of the rope, inching his way steadily further out across the river. After several minutes of gruelling effort, he was at last able to feel the riverbed beginning to slope upwards in front of him. Struggling to regain his footing, he staggered out of the water on to the opposite bank and then lay there with his chest heaving until the biting cold drove him to his feet. He used the rope to haul their clothes and kit across, rubbed himself down vigorously with his shirt, putting some warmth back into his body, and then pulled his clothes back on before readying himself to haul Ahmad across.

Now that Shepherd was on the far bank, it was a much more straightforward task to get Ahmad across. With the rope firmly attached around his waist, Ahmad waded out into the river. Although the current again swept him off his feet, Shepherd's secure footing on the opposite bank made it an easy matter for him to pull on the rope and drag Ahmad across. Once they were re-united, Ahmad dressed quickly and then they set off back along the bank towards the enemy position.

CHAPTER 7

The day had started normally for the soldiers who were defending the bridge. The night sentry had woken them before dawn, when they carried out their ritual wash before performing their morning prayers. After that they cooked and ate their breakfasts and then settled down for yet another boring day watching the bridge, already convinced that nothing would happen. If their experience of the previous couple of weeks was anything to go by, the most exciting thing that they could expect to occur would be the arrival of an occasional old man or young boy taking a scrawny collection of goats across the bridge, making for the mountain pastures where they would spend the spring and the brief Afghan summer.

What happened a couple of hours after first light took them by surprise. A white-skinned Westerner holding an AK-47 rifle appeared as if from nowhere a few hundred yards in front of them on the opposite side of the river. The sentry stood stupefied for a few seconds, doubting the evidence of his eyes, but then he shouted a warning – 'Ingreesi! Ingreesi!'

and started to crank the cocking handle of the heavy machine gun to arm it.

Jock, Geordie and Jimbo had spent most of the previous night digging shell scrapes at their firing positions. The only tools that they had were their personal fighting knives and this had made the job painstakingly slow. As dawn approached they had retreated into the coffin shaped holes they had made and listened as the troops across the river slowly began their daily routine. The three of them could hear and smell everything that was happening and Geordie, who like the others, had had nothing to eat for three days apart from his belt rations, could hear his stomach rumbling as the smell of the food drifted across the river towards him.

'Bloody hell, Geordie,' Jimbo whispered. 'Keep it down will you, your guts are making enough noise to be heard in Kabul.'

'Yeah, well unlike you I'm not carrying several pounds of fat to get me through lean times,' Geordie hissed back.

Jock waited until it was full light and then, summoning up all of his resolve, he took a deep breath and stood up in full view of the sentry. The whole team had agreed that they would have to give the enemy enough rope to make their intentions clear, because it was just possible that they were guarding the bridge for some other reason, totally unconnected to the Brits' presence. There was an outside chance that they wouldn't open fire but once they had done the SAS men would feel able to retaliate.

Jock had worked out the odds as shrewdly as any professional poker player and he watched calmly as the sentry armed the heavy machine gun, swung the barrel to point towards him and then loosed off the first couple of rounds. Nervous and probably over-excited, the sentry's aim was well off and, just as Jock had expected, the first burst of shots flashed harm-lessly past him, passing high overhead before shred-ding the foliage of a pine tree on the lower slopes of the hillside behind him. Having satisfied himself that the sentry and his fellow-soldiers had shown no signs of wanting to be friendly, Jock killed the sentry with a clinical double tap from his AK-47 before slid-ing back into his shell scrape. Had anyone wanted to ask him about it, Jock would not have regarded what he had just done as being particularly brave. From his long experience in war zones all over the world, he knew that Soviet-made machine guns were notori-ously inaccurate even when fired by men far more skilled in their use than a jittery young Afghan sentry, who had probably never fired anything bigger than a rifle in anger before. He doubted that the sentry would have been able to have hit the proverbial barn door, at least not with the first few shots. But offer-ing himself up as a sitting duck wasn't something he planned to do again anytime soon.

The other Afghan soldiers, who had been lounging around the armoured personnel carrier a few seconds before, smoking and drinking mint tea, scrambled for their weapons and tried to return fire, but the three SAS men were now bringing a storm of witheringly accurate fire to bear on them. Jimbo and Geordie's lines of fire had been precisely calculated to herd the survivors towards the armoured personnel carrier.

Panicking and terror-stricken, the defenders were unwittingly co-operating wholeheartedly with the SAS men, because those of them who were still breathing were running flat out to get into the armoured car before any more of them were cut down. However, although the Afghan soldiers could shelter from the incessant fire inside the personnel carrier's armoured interior, just as the SAS men had hoped, the body of the dead sentry was blocking their access to its main gun.

While Geordie and Jimbo were keeping the enemy soldiers occupied, Jock had been taking a series of carefully aimed shots at the steel nose cone of the Spigot rocket on the turret of the armoured personnel carrier. After half a dozen near misses, each one striking sparks from the nose section and then ricocheting away, Jock hit the bullseye – the arming mechanism of the rocket – with his seventh shot. There was a blinding flash of light and a heart-beat later, a roar like a clap of thunder as the rocket exploded, sending white-hot shrapnel scything through the men around the vehicle.

It was the signal that Shepherd and Ahmad had been waiting for, and in the same instant that they heard the explosion, they broke cover and sprinted out of their hiding place a couple of hundred yards from the armoured personnel carrier. Although he could hear the rounds from his comrades' rifles cracking through the air around him, Shepherd knew that they would be perfectly safe if they kept the vehicle between themselves and the three other SAS men. It was the sole reason that Shepherd had spent so much time selecting the firing positions, thus ensuring that the angles of fire would leave a narrow safe corridor through which he and Ahmad could reach the armoured personnel carrier, unharmed by the streams of rounds passing to either side of them. Ahmad had taken some convincing but within seconds he could see that Shepherd was right.

Several of the enemy troops had already been cut down by shrapnel from the exploding rocket or the relentless AK-47 fire that Jock, Geordie and Jimbo had been laying down, but Shepherd was sprinting to try and reach the bulbous rear doors of the armoured personnel carrier before the rest of the enemy soldiers could lock themselves inside. Even as he ran towards it, Shepherd was also double-tapping the fallen enemy troops sprawled on the ground in his path as he ran. Some of those he double-tapped were already dead before he shot them, but others might only have been wounded and the one unbreakable rule in a contact was that you never left an enemy at your back, unless you were sure they were already dead.

Slowed by the need to mop up the enemy, Shepherd was just reaching the armoured personnel carrier when he heard the clang as the doors were slammed shut and the tortured screech of metal on metal as the locks were rammed home. Cursing under his breath, he barely broke stride as he immediately switched to Plan B. He sprinted round to the side of the troop carrier, stooping below the sight-line of the firing port, where one of the enemy was firing bursts from his weapon blindly into nowhere. Shepherd waited until the firing stopped while the man inside paused to change magazines and then inserted the barrel of his own AK-47 into the firing port and loosed off a full magazine into the interior of the troop carrier. He could hear the rattling and whining sounds, slightly deadened by the thickness of the armoured steel walls, as his rounds ricocheted around inside the steel shell. The noises were echoed by the answering cries of terror and pain from the men trapped inside the troop carrier, as Shepherd's bullets struck home. Tumbling in flight, but still travelling at deadly velocity, each round that hit one of the enemy soldiers punched an outsized, jagged hole in his flesh.

While Shepherd had been pouring fire through the aiming slit, Ahmad had been clambering on to the roof of the personnel carrier. He eased the body of the dead sentry out of the way enough to allow him to drop a hand grenade through the cupola into the turret of the vehicle. He used the seven seconds before the grenade detonated to push the body back down, blocking the gap, and ensuring that the body would tamp the charge so that all the explosive force was directed downwards. All that he heard as he crouched on the roof of the troop carrier was a dull thudding sound as the grenade exploded. Even if anyone had escaped the carnage caused by Shepherd's prolonged burst of rounds through the firing slit, they could not possibly have survived the blast and the shrapnel from a grenade detonating at a maximum of a handful of feet from them.

Shepherd was now satisfied that the area was safe He flashed Geordie a thumbs up and Geordie leapt out of his shell scrape dashed to the bridge. He began carrying out a quick search and soon found a demolition charge placed on the underside of one of the main struts. Within seconds he had disarmed it and dropped it into the river, where the current carried it harmlessly away downstream. He turned and gave a thumbs up to Jock and Jimbo as they emerged from their own shell scrapes. Still keeping a wary eye out for enemy troops who might have been in hiding further away, they crossed the bridge while Ahmad called to his men to follow them.

The welcome that Shepherd gave his comrades was less warm than they might have expected. 'What the fuck were you playing at, Geordie?' he said, his face showing his fury. 'If that demolition charge had gone off while you were fiddling with it, we'd have been looking for bits of you all over the mountainside.

'Yeah, sorry to alarm you, Spider,' Geordie said, though his smile suggested that he didn't take Shepherd's concern entirely seriously. 'I only did it for the old man,' he said, indicating Jock. 'We all know how much he hates water.'

Unlike Shepherd, Jock, who was a poor swimmer and had a morbid fear of drowning, was in no mood to criticise Geordie for what he'd done. 'The Newcastle Browns are on me when we get back to the big H,' he said, beaming at him. 'Even though we all know it's cat's piss anyway.'

CHAPTER 8

There were no more pitched battles as they carried on across country, skirting well wide of Kabul and travelling through the mountains to avoid the main road connecting the capital with the Panjshir Valley. Nonetheless, it continued to be a very fraught passage as they neared the valley, because the whole country seemed to be like an overturned beehive. Whenever they came to a settlement or one of the remote chai khana – tea houses – Shepherd and his comrades went to ground, concealing themselves in whatever cover they could find while Ahmad and his men walked on ahead and spoke to the locals or eavesdropped on the conversations in the tea house. Rough-built without the use of mortar or a single nail, the drystone walls of the tea house were roofed with long branches and sticks held in place by large flat stones. Animals were penned at one end of the long single room, filling the air with the smell of wool and dung, and sharing the space with men huddling around the fire of wood and dried animal droppings, where the samovar was always bubbling. Women travelling with their men were screened from the eyes of strangers by a filthy curtain stretched across one corner.

For centuries the tea houses had offered food and shelter to weary travellers and traders crossing the country, but they had also always served as clearing houses for news of bad weather, avalanches and tribal fighting, and for gossip and rumour, and in every place Ahmad and his men heard the same wild tales.

There were constant rumours and counter-rumours, not just of the tribal and factional fighting that had been going on unbroken ever since the Soviets were driven out of Afghanistan, but also of gangs of marauding faranji kafir – foreign infidels – and of the advances and retreats of the troops attempting to intercept them. Some of the wilder stories may even have been fuelled by the SAS mens' fight at the bridge, for no one knew who had wiped out the soldiers stationed there and in the absence of facts, ever stranger rumours kept being circulated and solemnly believed. However, some of the tales were rooted in fact. Itinerant merchants and pedlars moving through the countryside were reporting that they had encountered roadblocks on even the most minor tracks and groups of armed tribesmen were keeping watch over every bridge and ford. As a result, Ahmad and his men had to lead the SAS towards the Panjshir by way of an even more circuitous route than the one they would have liked and as a result, when they eventually arrived in the valley they were several days behind schedule.

The Panjshir Valley ran roughly south-west to north-east for 150 kilometres. They gave a very wide berth to the sprawling Bagram airbase at the entrance to the valley, where the Americans were continuing their massive military build-up. Helicopters were buzzing around the base like bees round a hive, and massive military transport aircraft – the familiar Hercules and the even more massive C-5 Galaxies that were big enough to airlift two Abrams battle tanks at once – were landing every two minutes. As they came in to land, their pilots punched out clouds of fierce white flares, burning like stars, to divert any heat-seeking missiles launched at them. As they taxied across the airfield, they passed ranks of rusting Migs and Tupolevs. Abandoned by the Soviets when they left, but spurned by the Taliban and now beyond repair, they had simply been bulldozed into an aircraft graveyard at the edge of the airfield and left to rot.

'Did you know Bagram was built with American money in the 1950s at the height of the Cold War?' Jock said. 'The Sovs used it after they invaded but now here we are, full circle forty-odd years later, with the Yanks back in charge again.'

Even though the Americans were Britain's closest allies and the SAS often worked with Delta Force on joint operations, on a "deniable" mission like this one it was essential that the SAS men avoided any contact with personnel, friendly or otherwise, who might unwittingly compromise their security or blow their cover. So with a wistful, sideways glance at the US base with its hot showers, PX stores and Pizza Hut outlets, the SAS men turned to follow Ahmad's men deeper into the Panjshir.

Barren mountain ranges rose on either side, with bands of parched grass and dry scrub alternating with screes and boulder fields. Lower on the slopes there were woods of cedar, larch, and pine cloaking some of the hillsides and copses of golden-leafed poplars alongside the river. The valley floor was covered in a patchwork of jewel-like small fields that were beginning to green with the spring planting. A handful of villages stood among the fields, the khaki-coloured mud brick houses nestling among the mulberry trees. The people working the land were mostly boys and old men – those of fighting age were probably otherwise occupied. Shepherd watched them using scrawny mules to drag wooden ploughs and harrows through the soil.

The river's torrents of icy meltwater, fed by the glaciers of the towering massif of the Hindu Kush that dominated the north-eastern end of the valley, were braided like plaits as they flowed around the mounds of boulders and the huge drifts of gravel washed down by each year's spring floods. The rusting remains of wrecked and long-abandoned tanks and military vehicles also punctuated the river bank at regular intervals, yet more souvenirs of the war with the Soviets and more recent battles with the Taliban.

Every time Shepherd raised his gaze, it was filled with a breathtaking vista of snow-capped mountain summits, stretching to the horizon. 'It's beautiful, Ahmad,' he said, as they stood on the ridge, looking down at the valley floor stretching away from them into the distance, 'and so peaceful.'

Ahmad inclined his head. 'It is a beautiful country, but do not be deceived by its quietness. We are a warlike people for good reason. Emeralds and silver have been mined here since the earliest times and they have always attracted thieves and warlords. The Panjshir is also a great trading route, the gateway to Central Asia, and has been fought over for thousands of years. The armies of Alexander the Great marched through this valley on his quest to conquer the plains of Asia and the rivers of the Indus. Timur, "The Sword of Islam", also marched through the Panjshir. He was a cruel conqueror who built towers and pyramids from the skulls of his enemies.' He gave a cold smile. 'The Red Army tried to as well, but unlike their predecessors, they did not get any further.'

'I'd already guessed that,' Shepherd said, 'just from the number of rusting Russian tanks we could see along the banks of the river.'

'Then, after the Soviets, there were the warlords and the Taliban,' said Ahmad. 'I cannot remember a night throughout the time when I was growing up here that was not punctuated by the sound of gunfire and explosions.'

'Can't have been easy, for a kid.'

'It wasn't easy for any of us,' said Ahmad. 'But we never gave up hope. We never surrendered. This is our country and we will fight for it for ever, until death if that's necessary.'

As they were about to move on, they paused to watch some small boys flying kites, their vivid shades of scarlet, purple and yellow, etched against the snow-capped mountains and the deep blue of the sky. 'Before the Taliban came to power,' Ahmad said, 'you would have seen such kites everywhere. They were our national passion, flying in thousands over the skyline of Kabul and Qandahar. But, like television, music, books and magazines, and the cage-birds which brought song and colour to our homes, kites were banned by the Taliban and anyone found with one was flogged with whips or electric cables. The Taliban are gone now, but still few Afghan children fly kites anymore.' He shuddered. 'I don't think anyone could understand how much my people hate the Taliban and everything they stand for,' he said.

As they moved on further into his home valley, Ahmad became visibly more relaxed and his men more elated. Instead of avoiding the villages, they now passed straight through them and in each one, as soon as the small boys keeping watch on the village outskirts saw them approaching, they ran to alert their fathers. The village elders then formed a welcoming committee, touching their hands to their hearts as they uttered the traditional Muslim greeting 'Salaam alaikum' and then embracing Ahmad and his honoured guests, the SAS men, and showering them with offers of rest, food and drink. It took longer to refuse than to accept. In almost every house they entered, sugar was ladled into cups placed before them and black tea poured into it, while they were offered bread or raisins, or sometimes the hot food that the house owner's wife had prepared for her family to eat. There was always a picture of Ahmad Shah Massoud too, placed in a niche or alcove like a shrine, with objects arranged in front of it like offerings to a god. Among the offerings from these warlike people were knives with blades stained with the blood of enemies, and spent bullets.

'What's with the bullets?' Jimbo asked, nodding at one display.

'They're a powerful talisman,' Jock said, still revelling in his role of local expert. 'A spent bullet extracted from a wounded man is supposed to protect the wearer from gunfire.'

Peaceful though the valley now seemed, signs of the fighting that had engulfed the country for decades were everywhere. There were gaps in the rows of houses where shelling or bombing had reduced dwellings to dust and rubble that still lay unrepaired, and the facades of those that still stood were marked like smallpoxed faces by the scars left by bullets and shrapnel. The village mosque must once have been completely covered in a mosaic of beautiful azure-blue tiles, but gun- and shell-fire had also hit the mosque and parts of the walls were now of clumsily repaired mud-brick, while many of the tiles lay in fragments, sparkling like jewels among the rubble at the foot of the wall. As everywhere in Afghanistan, there was another visible legacy of the country's warlike past and present: amputees were everywhere, and a high proportion of them were boys.

Ahmad followed Shepherd's gaze as he looked at one small boy, a double-amputee, helping his father at a roadside stall, selling the staples of Afghan life: rice, naan bread, black and green tea, and sugar. 'Many boys lost their limbs after the Taliban expelled all foreigners including the charities clearing the minefields,' Ahmad said. 'The Taliban set boys to do the job instead, crawling out over the fields holding sticks and knives which they had to push into the soil. No one knows how many were killed, but thousands were wounded and survived.'

When they eventually reached Ahmad's home village, the welcome was even more emotional and prolonged. Ahmad excused himself to visit the family women – no faranji kafir would be allowed to meet them – but he was back within an hour and they then went into an immediate congress with the tribal leaders of what remained of the Northern Alliance, almost all of them members of the late Massoud's vast extended family.

Ahmad interpreted for them as the leaders took it in turns to pour out a litany of complaints and grievances. 'After the death of Ahmad Shah Massoud, blessed be his name,' Ahmad said to Shepherd, translating the words of one venerable, white-bearded elder, 'the people of the Panjshir retreated back into the valley and kept themselves to themselves, but that was not because we were afraid, only because we were tired of fighting battles and wars for other people.'

The old man bared his teeth before speaking again. Ahmad waited until he had finished before translating 'However, let any enemy treat that as a sign of weakness and come into the Panjshir and they will see how we fight to defend our land and our people, just as we have fought those carrying out the recent attacks.'

The other elders queued up to echo his bitter complaints to Ahmad and the SAS men. The inhabitants of the valley, who were a rich mix of origins and ethnicities, were now being constantly provoked and goaded by incessant shelling and hit and run attacks, though none of them knew who was behind it, nor why.

'The enemies we captured have talked, of course,' another leader said via Ahmad. 'They thought that it might save their lives or at least earn them a quicker death, but even so, they had no knowledge of who was behind the attacks, nor what the motive for them might have been. The men who carried out the attacks were soldiers for hire – mercenaries you would call them – Pushtuns from Helmand and other provinces, who were given money and told what their targets would be, but nothing more.'

Ahmad had housed the SAS men in one room of his family house, a large, black-beamed, wood and mud-brick structure in the heart of the village. Like the other houses, its architecture reflected the region's troubled past and present. The face that it offered to the street was unbroken at ground floor level except for a stout oak door, studded with iron, and small, barred windows set high up in the walls, so that the occupants could look down on those outside and fire at them if necessary without exposing themselves to danger.

That evening the SAS men were given the first hot food they had eaten since leaving Peshawar. A curry made from some unidentifiable meat, flat bread, goats cheese and fruit. When they had finished eating, like their hosts, they sat with their hands spread, palms upward, while Ahmad said Grace, thanking Allah for the food they had eaten. The mujahideen then wiped their hands clean on their beards and turbans.

The pleasure the SAS men had taken from the hot food soon faded, when Jimbo, who as patrol signaller had been testing the communications, reported a major problem. The Northern Alliance used elderly, but normally reliable, radio equipment. It worked by using a transmission key to send Morse code dots and dashes, with the sender anglicising local dialect words and the receiver decoding them. It was a system which the British had used in its military outposts around the Middle East for decades, but for reasons that were not immediately apparent, the radio link between the Panjshir and Peshawar had now ceased to function. The British-trained mujahideen who operated the set was puzzled because it appeared that the radio was operating normally yet it now stubbornly refused to receive transmissions from Pakistan.

'Give me a couple of hours with it and hopefully I will be able to sort it out,' Jimbo said, but eventually, after wrangling with it for far longer than that, he had to admit defeat. 'I can reconfigure the set and build a dipole aerial for it,' he said. 'But I can only communicate to Hereford with the One Time Pad we were given. I might be able to hit the cell in Oman or Cyprus, but they won't be able to decipher our messages because the only other copy of the OTP is held in the Head Shed. They will be able to relay them to Hereford. We'll have to keep the messages short because the OTP method is pretty unwieldy but at least the system should be workable.'

It took him into the next day before he was able to send and receive messages to and from their headquarters. The explanation for the radio silence from Peshawar was soon forthcoming. The Head Shed told them that the safe house in Peshawar had been attacked by a massive car bomb. The building had been destroyed and its occupants – the Scaleybacks who had ignored Geordie's warning – had all been killed in the blast.

While advocating caution, the Head Shed stopped short of recalling the patrol, signing off with a last terse message 'Futints at yr discretion'.

'So what are our future intentions?' Geordie asked Shepherd, having studied the message.

'Well, it was a hell of a long, hard slog to get this far,' Shepherd said. 'It seems a pity to waste all that effort. We've got weapons, a relatively safe base area here and communications, so if the situation deteriorates we can decide at any time to pull the plug and exfiltrate.' He paused, glancing around the circle of faces. 'So for what it's worth, my vote would be to carry on with the mission.'

There was an instant chorus of 'Agreed' from the other three.

CHAPTER 9

Shepherd and his mates quickly set about training a cadre of the brightest and the bravest mujahideen in Special Forces tactics and philosophy, while Ahmad shadowed Shepherd everywhere acting as an interpreter. Some of the training proved to be pretty straightforward, because the mujahideen had an instinctive feel for the use of ground and could cover huge distances very quickly, as their fathers had demonstrated to devastating effect in their guerrilla war against the Soviet invaders. However, this was counter-balanced by the mujahideen being impulsive and impetuous in their decision making, and they were often easily distracted from the task in hand.

Shepherd and the others had repeatedly drummed into them the special forces' axiom of "the right force, with the right weapons, in the right place, at the right time". They also taught them the crucial importance of accurate reporting, target reconnaissance and targeted attacks. The mujahideen learned how to prepare explosive charges and how to make use of them in sophisticated attacks, how to avoid enemy troop concentrations and how a very small force could inflict proportionately heavy damage on the enemy.

The lack of adequate maps and radios was a hindrance but the SAS team taught the mujahideen how to make representative maps to scale and, probably most importantly in terms of planning and carrying out attacks, how to convey information logically and rationally. They also taught them a modified RV system that could be used to bring together several small groups into one large group for an attack, but which could also be used to allow a large group to break down into a number of smaller units to escape after a run-in with the enemy.

The SAS team had been feeling reasonably well pleased with the results of the training, but any complacency was shaken out of them one morning when they heard a familiar sound – the whistle of an incoming shell. Shouting a warning, they hit the dirt as an artillery round landed in the valley, quickly followed by a salvo. Several shells exploded harmlessly in the fields but two of them struck the village itself with fatal consequences. One landed in the garden of a house at the edge of the village and, though the soft earth absorbed some of the blast as the shell detonated, the house partially collapsed and the owners, an old couple who had been sitting drinking a cup of chai on a bench in the garden were both cut apart by shrapnel and killed.

Another shell, fitted with a delay fuse, caused far worse devastation. It burst through the roof of the building used as the school near the heart of the village, smashed down through the floors of the building and came to rest in the cellar, where a group of the youngest children were making paper flowers. There was a second's pause, a metallic click and then the shell exploded. The force of the blast blew out the corner posts of the building, which then completely collapsed, entombing the teacher and the children in the ruins. Those who had not already been killed by the explosion and the shrapnel were now crushed by falling bricks and timbers. Frantic parents tore at the rubble with their bare hands, screaming their children's names, but there were no answering shouts or cries. By the time they managed to force a way through to the cellar, the cleared rubble heaped around it was marked with bloodstains from the torn and bleeding fingers of the men and women who had dug their way into it, but their efforts had been in vain; the teacher and all eleven children lay dead. The heart-breaking sound of the women's funeral keening continued throughout the night.

The SAS team had been running an OP exercise that day and the mujahideen had been deployed in the peaks around the valley. 'Whoever is on the other end of that artillery must have been firing blind,' Jock said, 'because otherwise our guys up on the tops would have seen a forward observation party.'

Shepherd nodded. 'Get the guys back and make it quick. We're going to make these bastards pay for what they've done.'

Geordie fired a coloured flare – the recall signal for the mujahideen manning the OPs – and they soon began arriving back in the village. Shepherd allowed them only a few minutes to give vent to their grief and fury. 'You and your men have suffered a grievous loss here, Ahmad,' he said, 'but I know you will all be burning for revenge and we must move fast to achieve that. However it must be cool, calm and planned. Your wives and families will now take cover in caves and sangers, just as they have done for centuries when under attack, so there should be little further immediate risk to them from the shelling, but we need to destroy that artillery and kill or capture the men firing it.' He paused, studying Ahmad's face.

Ahmad nodded. 'We will do whatever it takes,' he said. 'Just tell us what we need to do.

'All right, first we need a report from each group of anything they've seen.'

Ahmad spoke to his men, he listened to their replies and then translated for Shepherd. None of the first OP groups to return reported seeing anything out of the ordinary, but when the last four mujahideen arrived back, they reported that they had spotted a column of a dozen heavy guns deployed in a shallow valley to the south-west of the Panjshir. Under questioning they described what Geordie quickly realised were self-propelled, tracked artillery pieces.

'Its bound to be ex-Soviet kit,' Geordie said. 'There are two types: the SP-152 and the SP-122. The bigger gun has a range of about twenty kilometres using normal charges or a few clicks more firing rocket-assisted projectiles, so that's probably why we didn't hear them firing.'

'Though the range will be less than that in these mountains,' Shepherd said, 'because the barrels will have to be elevated like howitzers.'

'True,' Geordie said. 'One other thing for your men to watch out for, Ahmad, is the remote-controlled heavy machine gun the SP-152s carry.'

Ahmad nodded and translated for his men.

'Okay Ahmad,' Shepherd said when he had finished translating, 'it's time to see if all that training's been worthwhile or wasted. You need to get your men to put together a couple of dozen standard charges as quickly as possible, using sticks of plastic explosives but with a detonating mechanism fitted at either end, so that they can either be used in one piece or cut into two halves.'

It took the mujahideen only a few minutes to make the charges and by the time they had done so, Shepherd and his SAS comrades had come up with a viable plan and he was ready to brief the group.

'You'll run this operation Ahmad,' Shepherd said, 'because speed is of the essence and if we go with you, we will only slow you down.' He noted Ahmad's quiet smile at the vote of confidence in him. 'We will follow up in the rear. Remember what we taught everybody about explosive placement and cannibalisation. The charges must be laid in the same place on every gun or piece of equipment to stop the enemy cannibalising them for spares and getting some of them back in action. Use the group who spotted the artillery pieces as your guides and leave one behind to bring the others along. Plan on making your attack at first light and please stress to them all that, though they must be thirsting for revenge, as the old saying goes, revenge is a dish best taken cold. One other thing: we need intelligence, which means that we need prisoners. By all means kill most of them, but try not to kill all of them. We need intel and dead men don't talk. Now good luck and get on with it.'

They all set off at the same time but with the phenomenal speed that they could maintain over their native mountains, the mujahideen were soon disappearing into the distance with the SAS men trailing in their wake.

Shortly after midnight, Shepherd and the other SAS men reached a ridge overlooking the valley where the enemy guns were sited. Using binoculars and night vision goggles, Geordie confirmed that the guns were indeed Russian SP-152s. The troops manning them were making little attempt to hide themselves, and the SAS men could see them sitting around their campfires, cooking and chatting, probably feeling safe from attack so far from their targets. However, no matter how hard the SAS men scanned the slopes and ridges around the gun-site, they could see no sign whatsoever of the mujahideen. 'Either our boys have given up and gone home,' Jock said, 'or they're even better at concealment than we thought.'

'We'll find out at first light which it is,' Shepherd said. Leaving Jock and Jimbo on the ridge to man the RV, Shepherd and Geordie began descending the slope towards the valley bottom. A couple of hundred feet above the valley floor they hit a scree slope made of small slate stones. 'Hell's bells,' Shepherd said, 'it's like being back on the Welsh Mountains again.'

'Yeah and in which case, that'll be Snowdon over there,' Geordie said, jerking a thumb towards the massive, snow-capped mountains of the Hindu Kush rising in the distance behind them. They knew from previous bitter experience that it would be impossible to descend further without causing landslides and alerting everybody in the area, so they found themselves a fire position and settled in comfortably to await developments.

As dawn broke there was a series of muffled thumps and flashes from the direction of the guns. On each gun they could see two explosions, one in the area of the driving sprockets on the tracks and another where the gun entered the turret.

'Our guys are good,' Geordie said, 'not only have they stopped the guns from being cannibalised and moved, they've also tried to distort the barrels. It doesn't get much better than that, does it?'

'Don't sound so surprised,' Shepherd said. 'They were taught by professionals.'

When Ahmad and his troops arrived back at the RV they were jubilant and over-excited at the success of the raid, but Jock calmed them down at once. 'The job's not done till the job's done,' he said. 'We don't start celebrating until we're sure that everyone is safe and accounted for. The first task is to do a body count, a Wounded In Action check and an ammo count. Remember your drills and what we've been teaching you. Check everybody out and we don't move until Spider and Geordie are back here as well.' The men nodded and went about their tasks.

In the dim light immediately after the first explosion, Shepherd and Geordie had spotted a couple of men wearing civilian clothes make a panic-stricken dash out of the camp towards them. As the pair hit the screes, in their fright and haste they started scrambling on all fours, trying but failing to make much headway up the slope and slithering back repeatedly as the loose rock moved beneath them.

Maintaining silence, Shepherd indicated by hand-signals to Geordie that, though they would take the pair out, he wanted them alive. As soon as Geordie had given the thumbs up to show he understood, Shepherd launched himself into space and landed on one of the men. He sensed rather than heard Geordie land on the other guy a fraction of a second later. Shepherd's man was winded by the impact, but the SAS man still gave him a "Don't argue" short-arm jab to his nose and a forearm smash across the throat, just to rule out any thoughts he might have had about escaping. After a short, sharp struggle, both men had been subdued and Shepherd manacled their wrists with plastic cable ties.

They arrived back at the RV an hour later, pushing their prisoners along in front of them. They had said not a word to them all the way as they marched them over the ridge and back to the RV before leaving them with a group of mujahideen guarding them while they conferred with their comrades.

'Sorry we're late,' Shepherd said, 'but we and our new best friends had to detour around the screes to get here. Ahmad, why don't you see if you can get them to talk. But try not to damage them too much in the process.'

Ahmad nodded. 'If it was just us, we would have shot them out of hand.'

'I'm sure you would,' Shepherd said, 'but now you know that there are more ways than one of playing the game. And the winner is usually the one with the best intel.'

The prisoners' faces were contorted with fear as they saw the expressions of the mujahideen. They had been behind the shelling of the mujahideen village and killed several of their children and it was clear that only the mujahideen's obedience to Ahmad and the iron discipline instilled by their SAS trainers was holding them back from butchering the captives on the spot.

Unable completely to break the habits of a lifetime, Ahmad still slapped the two hapless prisoners around for a while but then began shouting a volley of questions at them in the guttural Pushto language. After questioning them for a few minutes, he turned back to Shepherd. 'They won't say much,' he said. 'They keep saying their innocent but of course that's a lie. They are convinced that if they admit to shelling the village we'll kill them on the spot.' He snarled. 'Which is probably how this is going to end because I don't see my men allowing them to live, not after what they've done.'

'They're not local, are they?'

Ahmad shook his head. 'The dark one's a Pakistani, the other's an Iranian. They make unlikely bedfellows, don't you think?'

'They certainly do,' Shepherd said, exchanging glances with Jock. 'We may just have hit pay-dirt here, so we'll take them back to the Panjshir with us and see what more they have to say for themselves there.'

'My men won't like that,' said Ahmad.

'You have to explain to them that they must talk first. What happens after that I couldn't care less about. But you have to keep your men in check until we have finished interrogating them.'

Ahmad nodded. 'They will talk,' Ahmad said, 'you should have no fear of that. If they don't, we will skin them alive.'

Shepherd smiled tightly but he had to suppress a shudder. He had seen more action than even the most battle-hardened Afghan fighter but talking casually of flaying a man alive like some barbaric mediaeval ritual struck a chill into his heart. He had huge respect for the courage, endurance and fighting skill of Ahmad and his men but there were parts of the Afghan psyche that he would never understand.

CHAPTER 10

Before setting off back over the mountain to the Panjshir, Shepherd gave detailed, specific instructions to Ahmad on how the two prisoners were to be handled. 'They are to be separated from each other and then taken back to the valley by a circuitous route, with only a couple of your men as guards for each of them,' Shepherd said. 'They are to be kept manacled and gagged, so they can neither talk to their captors, nor to each other. If they attempt to escape, they are to be recaptured and then they must be shackled or hobbled with ropes, even if that means that they are continually falling and hurting themselves. But most important of all, Ahmad, the handlers must not talk to the prisoners at all and must ignore them as far as possible. They should avoid touching, making eye contact or helping the prisoners in any way during the trip back. Once in the Panjshir, they are to be blindfolded and their ears blocked, so they can neither see, nor hear anything.'

'I understand,' said Ahmad.

'I know you do, but your men must too,' said Shepherd. 'I need you to come back with me, so your men will be in sole charge of the prisoners. I don't want anything happening to them in your absence.'

'I will explain to them,' said Ahmad. 'Don't worry. The prisoners will not be harmed. Not yet, anyway.'

'That's going over the top, don't you think?' asked Jock as Ahmad went over to talk to his men.

Shepherd shrugged. 'You think? Do you remember the resistance to interrogation training ops we used to do when the prisoner handlers were Gurkhas? Most of them didn't speak English or any other language that their prisoners were likely to recognise anyway, and they treated all of us just like packages, which was exactly how the interrogators had taught them and how they liked it done. Everybody and everything was neutral, so that when our turn came to be interrogated, we had nothing to focus on other than the guy in front of us and the questions he was asking. The way the Gurkhas did the job cut out most of the weaknesses in the system and made it much harder for us to indulge in fantasies about escaping or hope that telling some bullshit story would gain us an advantage. That's what I'm hoping to replicate here.'

Jock grinned. 'Psyops?'

'Call it what you want,' said Shepherd. 'We have got to keep them mentally off balance, with their senses diminished. At this moment they think we will kill them out of hand.'

112

'With good reason,' Jock said. 'Ahmad and his men would have topped them already, given half a chance.'

'Exactly,' said Shepherd. 'If they keep believing that then they'll retreat inside themselves to try to make their peace with whichever God they believe in. But if they think they can buy their lives with information, they will say anything that they think we want to hear, so if we can keep it neutral instead, it should make things easier for us later on.'

While the prisoners and their escorts made their slow, circuitous way back to the Panjshir valley, Shepherd and the others hurried back there. As soon as they arrived at the Massoud clan's headquarters, Shepherd took Ahmad on one side. 'We need your help again, Ahmad, to set up the next phase,' he said. 'We need a three-roomed building, or part of a larger building will do, but the rooms must have interconnecting doors, and each room must be small enough so that a conversation in one room can be heard in both of the others.'

Ahmad thought for a moment and then nodded. 'Give me a few minutes and I will arrange it.'

He returned within half an hour. 'I've found a house that I think will be suitable.'

'Is it unoccupied?'

Ahmad gave a wolfish grin. 'It is now. The owner was disposed to argue about it, but when he saw the look in my eye he fell silent instead and started packing his bags.'

He led Shepherd through the streets of the village before stopping at an ancient, mud-brick building. Like its neighbours, its architecture reflected the region's troubled past, with a heavy oak door and three tiny windows, little bigger than firing slits on the ground floor, and walls pock-marked by the impacts of rifle rounds. Upstairs, the windows were larger and there was what might have been a low-walled balcony or a firing platform at the eastern end of the building.

Ahmad ushered Shepherd inside. There were signs of the previous occupants' hasty departure in the still smouldering fire in the grate of the main room, and some half-eaten food congealing in a tin dish. Shepherd checked each room in turn. They were just as he had specified: small, interconnecting and with interior doors and walls flimsy enough for any sound to be readily heard from one end of the building to the other.

'This'll do fine, Ahmad, thanks,' he said.

'If there is anything else you need, you only have to name it.'

'As a matter of fact, there is one other thing: do you know of anyone who speaks Farsi?'

Ahmad smiled. 'Anyone apart from me, you mean?'

'Really? You speak it?'

'Like a native,' said Ahmad. 'Don't look so surprised. My people have been trading with the Persians since the days of Perseus and everyone in the Panjshir speaks the language, though we call it Dari, not Farsi. Pushto is the second language here.' He gave a bleak smile. 'It is yet another source of difference with the Taliban, who speak only Pushto, though about half of all Afghans still speak Dari. There are some differences from the Iranian version, including our accent, but just as you English can understand Americans, so we can understand Iranians.'

'So you actually speak English, Dari and Pushto?'

'And enough Urdu and Tajik to make myself understood in those tongues as well. But please don't misunderstand me, I'm not boasting, speaking several languages is not unusual here. In fact it's a necessity. After all, we live at one of the crossroads of the ancient world. It was a great trading route when your ancestors were still scratching in the mud.'

'To be honest now, that does sound a tad boastful,' Shepherd said with a sly smile.

Ahmad laughed. 'Only about the Panjshir Valley, not about myself.'

Together with Ahmad, the four SAS men embarked on a long, detailed discussion about the best strategy to adopt when interrogating their prisoners. When all had had their say, Shepherd summarised the main points and re-briefed the team on the strategy they had agreed, to make sure there were no errors. 'Right,' he said, 'we all think the Pakistani guy is almost certainly a member of the ISI – the military Inter-Services Intelligence Group from Islamabad. Although the group draws its members from the Army, Navy and Air Force and he isn't wearing any badges of rank, it's a fair bet that he's an army officer because the army effectively controls the organisation. If that turns out to be correct, it's almost certain that he speaks and understands English.'

'He understands English all right,' Geordie said. 'Did you see the way he looked at us when we were talking, just after we put the cuffs on him?'

'If he understood your version of English he must be a fucking cunning linguist,' Jock said. 'I can barely understand half of what you say.'

'This from a fucking Scot?' said Geordie. 'They call it the Queen's English for a reason and that reason is the Scots can't bloody handle it.'

Shepherd tried to hide a smile. The everlasting Scots-Geordie rivalry between the two men kept them all entertained. 'Ladies, ladies, let's concentrate on the job in hand, shall we?' he said. 'Let's focus on our Pakistani friend. So, I think we can assume that he was educated at an army public school in Pakistan. That being the case it's probable he's also been trained in resistance to interrogation, or at the very least is familiar with the techniques. I say this because in the past few years there has been a great deal of cooperation and the sharing of ideas between the MOD, the Pentagon and Islamabad. I don't think they'll have refined our techniques very much. In fact I think they will have gone down the road of abusing and degrading any prisoners they've had their hands on, because to these guys, dishing out pain and punishment is the natural way to go, and they can't see, or don't want to see, that it's counter-productive.'

'They're fucking animals, that's what they are,' said Geordie. 'They wouldn't recognise the Geneva Convention if it bit them on the arse.'

Shepherd ignored the interruption. 'Now, we've been abused by professional sadists ourselves and we know that any Intelligence you extract under pressure can't be relied on or acted on, because people who crack under that sort of brutal treatment will say anything and agree to anything, irrespective of whether it's true or false, just to get the punishment to stop. So if it turns out that we're right, he is likely to be arrogant and cocksure. He will look down on the local tribesmen as mere peasants, and he will probably look down on us as well, once he realises that we're just trogs, not officers. On the other hand, the Iranian is probably a completely different case. I'm guessing he's an NCO with a good knowledge of artillery procedures, not an agent or an intelligence officer. That being the case I'm expecting that he'll only be able to fill in any gaps that the ISI guy leaves in his story. So initially we will concentrate on the Pakistani, even though we can expect the Iranian to crack first.' He looked at them one by one, checking that he had their full attention. 'Right, good luck guys and let's hope it all goes to plan.'

'Aye, there's a first time for everything,' Jock said, with a wink.

'Aren't you forgetting the old maxim: "No plan ever survives contact with the enemy",' Jimbo said.

'Well, maybe this will be the exception that proves the rule,' said Shepherd.

CHAPTER 11

The prisoners, each still gagged, manacled with cable ties and hobbled with ropes tied around their ankles so they could take no more than short, shuffling steps, arrived a few hours later, prodded along by two silent, glowering guards. They were dumped unceremoniously into the two rooms at opposite ends of the requisitioned building. They were left there, still manacled, with blindfolds over their eyes and their ears covered with pads of fabric held in place by cord wound so tightly around their heads that it bit into their skin.

'We'll let them stew for a while longer before we go to work on them,' Shepherd said. 'Let their fear do part of our work for us.'

The next day their guards removed the prisoners' blindfolds and ear coverings, but not the cable ties. As instructed, they worked in silence, ignoring all questions and requests and avoiding any eye contact with them. Once more, the SAS men stayed out of sight, leaving Ahmad's men to deal with the prisoners.

The following day the SAS team assembled in the middle room of the building and started to talk amongst themselves but in very low voices, using mostly slang and Jock and Geordie's rich mixture of dialects, so that although the prisoners could hear them talking, what they were saying would have made no sense to them. Finally Shepherd was ready to go to work on the prisoners. He strolled into the room where the Pakistani officer was being held.

Shepherd stood looking at him for a moment, then called out over his shoulder 'Why is this man still handcuffed, when you know he is an officer? Free him immediately and bring him a drink.'

Jock came running into the room, saluted Shepherd and said 'Yes Sir', and immediately hacked the cable tie from around their prisoner's swollen wrists.

Shepherd gave the officer a crisp salute of his own. 'I do apologise for the rough treatment. I'm afraid the local tribesmen aren't familiar with the Geneva Convention, and can get a bit out of hand.'

The prisoner squared his shoulders and began to harangue Shepherd and Jock. 'You're nothing but a rabble yourselves and a disgrace to the army, and I demand that you release me immediately.' He was in his thirties, dark skinned with a lustrous moustache and thick eyebrows that almost merged into one.

It was just the beginning Shepherd had hoped for. They had the Pakistani officer exactly where they wanted him: secure in the belief that he was their superior. Once he had calmed down, instead of sticking to the soldier's minimum disclosure under interrogation: name, rank and number, he proved to be quite happy to talk about military matters and his time at school in Quetta, and to speak vaguely about his army career. He was carefully building the foundations of the cover story that he hoped would convince them that he was simply a soldier following orders and that he shouldn't be blamed for the civilian deaths.

Shepherd also guessed that the Pakistani officer's superior attitude was because he was confident that the British soldiers would not get back to the UK alive. He was counting on them having to pass through Pakistan when they left the country, since all Afghanistan's other neighbours were hostile to Britain – and as soon as they set foot in Pakistan they would be dead men. A click of his fingers would be enough to seal their fate.

Ahmad meanwhile had quietly entered the other room and had given the Iranian some water and freed his wrists. He visited him several more times, each time without speaking a word to him, but whenever the indistinct sound of the others speaking English could be heard through the wall, he rolled his eyes at the Iranian and pointed towards the other room, trying to convey that he empathised with him and miming that by now, the Pakistani was good friends with his captors.

As Shepherd had hoped and expected, it was the Iranian who cracked first. Feeling isolated and betrayed by the Pakistani, he suddenly grabbed Ahmad's arm and said 'Do you know Farsi? Please, tell me what you want from me. I don't want to die in this pigsty.'

A few minutes later he was sitting in front of Shepherd and the rest of the team, spilling his guts, with Ahmad translating for him. 'I am a senior NCO in a Republican Guard artillery unit,' he said, via Ahmad. 'I'm an expert in the use of Soviet artillery equipment, which I learned during the war against Iraq. When invading Iraqi troops poured across our frontiers, we were all happy to answer the call to defend our homeland. We loved Imam Khomeini, and we went into battle with hearts filled with joy. After the revolution, the Americans and their stooges imposed an arms embargo on Iran but continued to supply Saddam Hussein with every kind of modern weapon.'

He fixed Shepherd with a cold stare. 'Saddam is your enemy now, but he was your friend then, even though he was just the same butcher. All we had was manpower and we attacked in waves, even into the mouths of Iraqi machine guns, and we were cut down in thousands. If we could not cut the Iraqi barbed wire, men would throw themselves on it with their bodies, so others could pass over us. Then I saw how unequal a war we were fighting, yet despite that, we kept fighting for eight long years. All we had was ourselves, while the other side had everything: artillery, aircraft, heavy weapons. What equipment we did have came from Afghanistan, sold to my country after being captured from the Russians. I learned how to lay and control artillery fire, and target the Iraqi dogs. We fought them to a standstill and we will do the same to anyone else – including the Great Satan, America – who attacks our homeland.'

Shepherd let the man talk until he had run out of steam. He passed him a plastic bottle of water and watched as he drank greedily. 'Yeah, that's all very sad and very patriotic,' Shepherd said, 'but we're not really interested in your history. All we want to know is what you are doing here and now in Afghanistan.'

'I was stationed in western Iran close to the Iraqi border, but six months ago, I was detached from my unit and sent to a proscribed military area to the east of Tehran, near the Birjand Mountains. Anyone who entered this area without permission was shot on sight.'

Shepherd leaned forward. 'And why was that? What was there?'

'I don't know exactly. There were two secret installations, one military the other civilian. I did not see or visit the civilian site, I only heard about it in barrack room gossip, but the military unit there was commanded by Colonel Farehdi of the Savama Secret Police. He is a really bad man. He brought me with him to Afghanistan.'

Hold it,' Shepherd said. 'This Farehdi is here?'

'He was with us at the gun site directing operations when we were firing the artillery into the Panjshir Valley, but he had left before you and your men attacked us. I don't know where he is now, probably on his way back to Iran.'

'So what was your role here?

'I was brought to help run some artillery here with the Pakistani officer, but I am only a gun layer for him, bringing the guns to bear on targets that the Pakistani officer selects. He is another really bad man and you should not believe what he says, just because he speaks English.'

Shepherd sat back and glanced around his comrades. 'Everybody happy?' He nodded to Ahmad, who took the Iranian back to the end room, leaving his wrists unmanacled. Some of his men then brought the Iranian some food and green tea while Ahmad returned to the middle room.

'Okay, Ahmad it's showtime,' Shepherd said. 'Do they know what to do?'

Ahmad gave a cold smile. 'Don't worry, they don't need any prompting from me.' He went out into the street and a few moments later they could hear the voices of the women, raised in an ululating chorus that was both a lament and a call to arms. Soft at first, it grew steadily louder and the lament gave way to an angry repetitive chant.

Jock stood up, kicked open the door to the room where the Pakistani officer was being held and dragged him roughly into the room. The other three SAS men stood in a semi-circle facing him, their expressions cold and hard.

'Right,' Shepherd said. 'It's time to cut the bullshit. We want to know everything about your friend Colonel Farhedi, what you are doing near the Panjshir Valley and what the connection is between the Pakistan and Iranian military. If you lie to us, hold back information or in any other way try to fuck us about, we will hand you over to that lot out there.' He paused for a moment and in the silence, they could all hear the eerie, flesh-creeping noise of the voices of the village women ululating outside; the sound was growing louder, harsher and more menacing with every passing moment.

Shepherd let the officer listen to it for a few more seconds before he spoke again. 'You realise that if we hand you over to them, they'll literally skin you alive, very slowly, in revenge for what your guns have done to their children?'

Their prisoner visibly paled at Shepherd's words, and began stammering out a few words of his own, trying to bargain with him, but the stone-faced SAS men offered him no possibility of compromise. 'I just told you,' Shepherd said. 'You have only one option: to talk and tell us the truth, or you will be handed over to the women.'

'You're bluffing,' the Pakistani officer said, though his voice cracked as he said it. 'We are all military men. I am an officer and you are English soldiers who are bound by the rules of war.'

Shepherd smiled. 'As you must already have noticed, we're neither officers nor English gentlemen, and where we come from and where we operate, there are no rules – of war or anything else. We work under a much older and simpler system: kill or be killed. It's your call. And frankly I don't give a fuck either way. I'm quite happy to let those women out there deal with you. I hear they cut off the dicks of men they kill and keep them as trophies.'

The sound of the women had been steadily growing louder, and was now almost deafening, a shrill, piercing clamour that sent chills even down Shepherd's spine, but still their prisoner made one last attempt to avoid his fate. 'I will not be treated like an animal,' he said.

Shepherd shrugged. 'Have it your way,' he said. He turned to Jock. 'Okay, looks like it's time to feed the hyenas.'

Jock and Geordie grabbed the officer's arms and started to drag him towards the door to the street. As they did so, his knees gave way, a damp stain appeared on the front of his trousers and a puddle began to form at his feet. 'All right, all right, I'll tell you what I can,' he said, the words running into each other.

In his terror the Pakistani officer gabbled so fast that what he said was partly garbled. 'I am a loyal soldier. Our military mission is to destabilise as much of Afghanistan as possible, so that other foreign powers will find it impossible to control or deal with the situation. My commanders believed that if we could fool the tribes in the Panjshir Valley into thinking their neighbours had carried out the shelling and provoke them into making revenge attacks on them, it would rekindle all the old hostilities and the whole country would go up in flames.'

All the time the ululating of the women was getting even louder and he kept shooting nervous glances towards the door as he spoke.

'So we know why you are here,' Shepherd said, 'but that doesn't explain the Iranian connection. What is Farehdi's role in all this?'

'Colonel Farehdi is a senior officer in the Iranian Intelligence Service, Savama. He had begun as a junior officer in Savak under the Shah but after the Iranian revolution in 1979, he transferred his allegiance from the Shah to the Ayatollahs. He is totally ruthless, a survivor. If anyone or anything gets in his way, it will be destroyed. Farehdi even bragged to me that he was the one who had paid for the assassination of Ahmad Shah Massoud. He had been with us at the gun site directing operations when we were firing the artillery into the Panjshir, but his survival instinct is very well developed and he left immediately afterwards, well before we were attacked by your Tajik friend's men.' He hesitated. 'That is all I know. I swear.'

'But you still haven't told us about the joint objectives of the Pakistanis and Iranians,' Shepherd said.

The prisoner's gaze again flickered to the door. By now the noise from the ululating women outside was deafening. 'Promise you will save me from them and I will tell you everything.'

Shepherd just shrugged. 'You're not in a position to negotiate terms or impose conditions. Just keep talking. The more you tell us, the better your chance of getting out of this with your dick in one piece.'

'We are selling them our expertise, that is all I know,' stammered the officer. 'Even if you give me to those women outside I can tell you no more than that.'

Jock shoved the Pakistani officer back into the end room and a couple of minutes later the team held a quick debrief. 'The only thing that Pakistan exports is manpower,' Jock growled. 'They make fuck all but trouble so what expertise of theirs would the Iranians be interested in, when they can make plenty of trouble by themselves without any help from outsiders?'

'Well, I think that's a fairly easy one,' Shepherd said. 'What have the Pakistanis got that everyone else in the region wants more than anything? They are a nuclear power after all.'

'Bloody hell,' Jock said. 'So what happens now?'

'I don't know yet, we need more time to think about it, but meanwhile we have to decide what we are going to do about this pair of arseholes that we're holding as prisoners.'

'We should keep the trog,' Jimbo said. 'He was just following orders from Farehdi and the Pakistani Rupert, and besides he might come in handy later on.'

'And the other one?'

'I dunno,' Geordie said. 'But one thing's for sure, we can't let him go.'

Jock shrugged. 'So toss him to the women then.'

'We will deal with him,' Ahmad said.

Shepherd frowned. 'I don't know about that, Ahmad. He did co-operate, after all.'

'What else are we going to do with him?' Jock said. 'I don't see we've many choices here.'

Ahmad folded his arms and gave Shepherd a hard stare. 'We respect you, your skill and your courage. You need to respect our ways and our justice. He has killed some of our children. For that he must die. Give him to me first to avenge my uncle and when I am finished with him, he can go to the women.'

'He's right, Spider,' said Geordie. 'This isn't our fight. We're not even here officially.'

'And he'd kill us in a heartbeat,' said Jock.

Shepherd looked over at Jimbo. 'He killed women and children without a second thought,' said Jimbo. 'I'm not going to babysit him from here on in. The guy has it coming. Ahmad deserves his revenge. They all do.'

There was a long silence but eventually Shepherd gave a slow nod. 'Very well then, take him,' he told Ahmad.

Ahmad grinned and hurried out before Shepherd could change his mind.

They could hear the Pakistani officer shouting, protesting and then begging as Ahmad and his men dragged him outside. It was the last time that the SAS men saw their prisoner, but an hour or so later the women's ululations rose to an even louder pitch and, half-buried by the sound, they heard an unearthly, high-pitched scream, and then another, and another.

'Bloody hell,' Geordie said, wincing at the noise. 'That Pakistani officer was a murderous arsehole, but I'm not sure that even he deserves what they are doing to him.'

'I won't be shedding any tears for him – he had it coming,' Jock said with an evil smile. 'But you can always go out there and try and reason with them, I'll be interested to see if you scream with a Geordie accent.'

CHAPTER 12

Ahmad reappeared some time later, and began talking to them as if nothing out of the ordinary had happened. Swallowing his reservations about the Pakistani officer's fate, Shepherd resumed the discussion about their next moves. As the sun was setting they broke off to eat a meal of kid goat and rice prepared by Ahmad's wife and mother, and then they lay, smoking and talking, on the flat roof of Ahmad's two storey house on the edge of the village. By now it was fully dark with an icy chill in the air, but they were in no hurry to move, enjoying the breathtaking panorama of the stars overhead, with the snow-capped peaks of the Hindu Kush still just visible, illuminated by the starlight and filling the eastern horizon.

'Do you believe in God?' Ahmad said after one long period of silence.

Shepherd and the others raised their heads in surprise. 'Blimey Ahmad, where did that come from?' Shepherd said.

'It was something I've been wondering about. So, do you – believe in God, I mean?'

'I was saying a while back, I've never yet met a soldier who didn't cry out to one God or another when the bullets start flying,' said Shepherd.

'There are no atheists in foxholes, that's what they say,' agreed Jimbo.

'Looking at the sky in the east, it is tempting to believe in something,' Shepherd said, 'Because right now I can see billions of stars and galaxies up there and it is easy to imagine that there must be some pattern, some purpose, or some supreme being up there. But in the grey light of northern Europe with a bunch of corrupt clergy fleecing and deceiving the faithful, it's much harder to believe in anything like that.' He paused, studying Ahmad's expression. 'But do you really mean, do I believe in a God to keep me safe in battle? Because if that is the real question, then the answer is no. My comrades and I believe in something, but it's not a supreme being blessing our actions because we think God is on our side.'

'You'd need to be talking to Delta Force for that, Ahmad,' Jimbo said. 'They're almost all born again Christians, who hold a prayer meeting before they go on any mission.'

'And they're good at what they do,' Shepherd said. 'But it's not the praying or the belief in God that makes them good. It's the training and preparation they do. And we're just the same.'

'In fact, we taught them everything they know,' Jock said, getting in on the act.

'The Taliban fight because they believe Allah wants them to fight,' said Ahmad. 'And they believe that Allah is on their side.'

'Well that I don't believe,' said Shepherd.

'I won't have anything to do with any God that forbids bacon,' said Jock, but Shepherd flashed him a warning look. Ahmad was a sworn enemy of the Taliban but he was a devoted Muslim, too.

'I don't believe that God is on my side when we go into combat,' said Shepherd. 'We believe in good professionalism, cool assessment of the risks and clear, coherent decision-making, and we rely on our training, our backgrounds and our self-belief. We're not kamikazes, troops with a death wish taking stupid risks for the adrenaline rush. If we don't believe that we can succeed, then we don't even start out on a mission. Those are the factors that keep us alive and make us successful, not praying in the heat of battle and losing focus on what needs to be done.'

Geordie cleared his throat. 'And probably the most important factor that we address is this: Know Your Enemy. If you do know your enemy, you can either force them or persuade them to follow a course of action which you can exploit. If you don't know your enemy, you are forever pissing into the wind. But to answer your question, I believe in a God, sure. But that's something very separate from being a soldier.'

Ahmad nodded. 'But you have beliefs, right? So what happens when you are not working

133

independently and just carrying out the orders of your superiors and those orders contradict what you believe in?'

Shepherd shrugged. 'We are soldiers and of course we carry out orders, but only if the orders make sense to us. A superior officer only commands the part of the battlefield he can see, and what he can't see, he tries to control by radio. But if he wants troops to fix bayonets and charge machine guns, then he's got to find somebody else to do it for him, because we would refuse to obey such a stupid order.'

'But if you refuse to obey an order, you could be court-martialled and even shot, couldn't you?

Jock smiled. 'I'd like to see them try. Trying to make us follow orders is why the Head Sheds want their troops wearing body and head cameras so that everything is streamed back to headquarters in real time.'

'Head Sheds?' repeated Ahmad, confused.

'That's what we call our commanders,' said Jock. 'See, they want to be able to sit in a totally safe environment and order others – us – to put our necks on the line for them. If you come back alive and haven't carried out their orders to the letter, then yes, you're looking at a court martial. So in that situation, the best solution is to break or lose your camera before the operation even starts.' He smiled. 'The bosses may be suspicious about it, but they can't prove anything and at least you will be alive.'

'And the mission has infinitely more chance of success,' Shepherd said, 'because it's been planned by the men with the skill and training, who actually have their boots on the ground.' He paused. 'Now enough of the theory and philosophy of war, let's get back to the real thing: the problems in hand. What are we going to do about the nuclear site in Iran? Because that's what it must be, mustn't it? There's no other explanation for what's going on.'

They began a Chinese Parliament, tossing in ideas and subjecting every suggestion to intense scrutiny and debate. They quickly defined their mission objectives. 'The first priority is to locate and severely damage or destroy this possible nuclear facility,' Shepherd said. 'The second priority – and it's a much lower one – will be to eliminate Colonel Farehdi, but only if an opportunity presents itself.'

'Oh no,' Ahmad said determinedly. 'The first priority must be the death of Farhedi. We have heard from the mouth of that Pakistani officer that Farehdi was the paymaster of the assassins of my uncle, Ahmad Shah Massoud. For that, I demand revenge. It is my right.'

Shepherd held up a hand to silence him. 'Ahmad, this is a team-driven operation. If you want to be part of it, you have to work as part of the team, and that includes carrying out any orders you're given and not going off on some maverick, vengeance-driven attack that could get us all killed and, even more important, jeopardise the main priority which has to be the destruction of that site. You and your men will definitely be of great help to us in achieving that aim, but if you don't want to go ahead on the basis that I've just outlined, it's better that you back out now, with no hard feelings on either side, and we'll go it alone instead.'

Ahmad looked as if he was ready to go on with the argument but then he took a deep breath and bowed his head. 'No, I want to be part of this mission. I will leave my vengeance on Farehdi on one side, until we have achieved your aims, and I will accept any conditions you impose and carry out your orders without question.'

Jock glanced at the others and rolled his eyes, because he was far from convinced of Ahmad's sincerity. Shepherd gave an almost imperceptible nod, to show he understood and shared Jock's concerns, but, speaking as much to his comrades as to Ahmad, he said 'I'm glad, Ahmad. Your knowledge of the terrain between here and the border and your ability to speak the Iranians' language will be very useful to us, and your bravery and fighting skills, of course. And I promise you, once we have taken care of the nuclear facility, you will get your revenge.' He paused. 'Right, let's get some serious planning under way.'

He reached under his tee-shirt and, with a slight ripping sound, he pulled out a large-scale map printed on silk that had been stitched to the inside. The map was a copy of an Air Ministry chart covering a large area of North and Central Asia. It was centred on Afghanistan, but also covered eastern Iran, the southern parts of what had once been the Soviet Union: Turkmenistan, Uzbekistan, Tajikistan and Kyrgyzstan, the Hindu Kush, a small slice of western China and part of Pakistan. These escape maps had been in use by Special Forces since World War II. They showed only major features such as mountains and lakes, and large population areas, and were not gridded like ordnance survey maps, being only intended to give an escapee a general direction to follow over a large area.

Like his comrades, the rest of Shepherd's escape kit was distributed around his body. There was a diamond-tipped, flexible wire saw in his waistband and a button compass sewn onto the fly of his trousers. He also had a flat knife blade that was concealed in the sole of his boot. It could be used as a throwing knife or as a sawing or cutting tool for butchering any birds or animals they managed to catch to supplement their meagre rations.

A quick glance at the map showed them how difficult this operation was going to be, as much because of the distances that they would have to cover, as the forces they might encounter while crossing hostile terrain and attacking what would inevitably be a well-defended target. From the Panjshir Valley to the Iranian border was a journey of 1200 kilometres and if what the Iranian NCO had told them was true, the Iranians' secret military and civilian sites were another 200 kilometres beyond that.

At Shepherd's direction, his team broke the operation down into a number of phases and carried out a broad-brush study to determine if the objectives were achievable.

Phase 1 would be the move from the Panjshir to the border.

Phase 2 would be to get from the border to the target area.

Phase 3 would be the target reconnaissance and attack.

Phase 4 would be the team recovery to Afghanistan or possibly Pakistan.

'Right,' Shepherd said, when they reconvened to discuss their findings. 'The first question is can the operation be done by vehicle? I don't want to walk unless we absolutely have to.'

Ahmad immediately dampened everyone's spirits. 'I'm afraid not, because it is impossible to cross the border covertly by vehicle.'

'Impossible isn't a word we use lightly in the SAS,' Geordie said. 'What's impossible for most people is all in a day's work for us.'

'In this case, it really is impossible,' said Ahmad. 'The border area is very dangerous. It is controlled by local tribes allied to the Iranians and although the people of the Panjshir Valley have been trading with Iran for a thousand years, ever since the Russian war the border has been virtually blockaded and no vehicles from outside the border area are ever allowed to cross into Iran. Anyone who wishes to trade with

Iran has to unload their vehicle and sell their goods at one of the many local markets on the Afghan side of the border, taking whatever prices they can get. The goods are then transported into Iran by the border tribesmen in their own vehicles and sold at a huge mark-up. There has been a long history of distrust between the border tribes and the people of the interior of Afghanistan and this situation and the recent fighting has only made the distrust and open hostility even worse. So if you wish to cross the border by vehicle, you will first have to defeat the combined forces of the border tribes, who number several thousand men.' He smiled. 'And as much as I respect your fighting skills, I doubt that even you are capable of that. However, what we can do is to hitch a lift on one of the many trucks that carry loads of goods through the Panjshir Valley and all the way to the border.'

'What sort of loads are there?'

'Everything. They carry produce, manufactured goods, and sometimes drugs and weapons too, many of which come down the Salang Highway from Russia or its former republics, and which are then traded in the border area to be sold on into Iran.'

'So that gets us to the border, or close to it,' Shepherd said, 'but we've still got to cover another 200 clicks beyond the frontier to reach the target area.'

'Which will take too long to cover on foot,' Jock said.

'We could use motorcycles,' Geordie said.

Jimbo's expression showed his reservations about that. 'We could, but the amount of fuel we would have to take will greatly restrict the amount of other operational kit that we can carry.'

They kicked around ideas for a few minutes longer before reluctantly coming to the conclusion that the mission could only be successful if they obtained a resupply inside Iran. 'And the only viable option for that,' Shepherd said, 'is an air drop.'

Geordie shook his head dismissively. 'There's no way on God's earth that the Head Shed are going to sanction a Herc overflying a hostile country. It wouldn't last ten minutes before the Iranians were blowing it out of the sky.'

'True, but I wasn't talking about a Herc. I was thinking of a fast jet coming in low and fast, dropping the resupply in dummy wing fuel tanks and then hitting the after-burners and getting the hell out of it again.'

'That could work,' Jock said. 'They could fit drogue chutes to the back of the tanks to lessen the impact when they hit the ground, but even so, they would still be going at a hell of a rate. So the contents would have to be really well cushioned or they would blow apart on impact like a bomb going off.'

Jimbo nodded. 'So it'll be interesting to see what they come up with for packing the contents.'

'But will the Head Shed and those up the line from them really be willing to risk an air asset like a

Tornado?' Geordie said. 'Particularly given the political fall-out if it gets shot down?'

'They will if it stops Iran from developing nuclear weapons,' Shepherd said. 'And if they don't want to use an RAF Tornado to fly below the Iranian air defence radars, they could always get one of the Saudi Air Force Tornados instead. And in any case, the Iranian air defence radars are mainly deployed around Tehran and the Iraqi border, not in the boon-docks where we're heading.'

'But will the Saudis really buy into it?' Geordie said, still sounding dubious.

'Why wouldn't they?' asked Shepherd. 'They hate the Iranians more than anyone. In fact the Saudis have a bigger stake in this than we do, because if the Iranians do develop nuclear weapons, you can bet that the second priority target after Tel Aviv will be Riyadh.'

He looked around the circle of faces, clocking the still sceptical expressions of a couple of them. 'Listen, one of the training operations to prove the efficiency of the Al Yamamah programme that earned BAE and the British government tens of billions was when a flight of Saudi Tornados carried out a simulated attack using their own aircraft to fly a mission of over 500 miles inside Saudi Arabia itself. The Saudi air defences were expecting them and were on full alert, but the only time the Tornados were detected was when they deliberately climbed high enough to allow themselves to be swept by the radar, just to prove they really were there. They dropped back down to low level and disappeared. And the Saudis had absolutely cutting edge Western technology at their disposal, whereas all the Iranians have is redundant Soviet kit. So if the Saudis couldn't detect their own Tornados flying at low level over their own terrain, I'm damn sure the Iranians won't be able to either. The Brits have enough clout with the Saudis to get them involved and we've seen enough of the Saudi pilots in action to know that they certainly have the skills to carry out the mission.'

'If I could just insert a quiet note of caution in all this?' Jimbo said. 'Can I remind everybody that to arrange something like this is pretty damn compli-cated and yet we are utterly reliant for comms on an antiquated Morse code radio as big as a bloody filing cabinet and the remainder of a one time code pad?'

'I know that,' Shepherd said, 'and I'm not under-estimating the difficulties, but if you use a combi-nation of one time pad code and plain language, it should simplify things a lot. Just code the secret stuff and send the non-sensitive in clear. And Jimbo? When you are ready to start sending, ask for "The Duck".'

'And who or what might The Duck be?'

'The Duck is a legendary cipher clerk whose real name is Donald, hence the nickname. All transmis-sions are automatically coded and decoded using computers, so a mixture of secure and non-secure in the same message would cause chaos in the system, but The Duck is so good that he'll be able to decipher our transmissions while simultaneously ordering a pizza on the phone and doing the Times crossword in his head. The guy's a genius. Literally. They say his IQ is bigger than Hawking's.'

He waited for a nod from Jimbo before continuing. 'Okay, we'll start by drawing up an outline plan for the air drop, and then a provisional kit list which we can amend once we've considered the various restrictions, distances, weight and time-frame involved. And Jock, remind them which edition mapping we are using, will you?'

Jock gave him one of his "exactly how dumb do you think I am" looks. 'Sure Spider, glad of the heads up on that. Shall I remind them that the sky is blue while I'm at it?'

Shepherd gave a rueful smile. 'Sorry, micro-management is my weakness, as you know. So the jet jockeys will be using two datum points which we must be able to identify on our rather crap maps. The first is likely to be something like a small airfield. They always have a beacon pumping out their identity electronically and usually with a flashing light doing the same in Morse, so that would make a readily identifiable start-point of the run in. The second datum point could be another small airfield or a distinctive geographical feature that will mark the end of the run. They will make the drop somewhere between those two points. They usually run along a compass heading in degrees, but we will have to ask them to do this run using mils instead. There are about eighteen mils to a degree so it is much more accurate from our perspective but correspondingly much more difficult for the pilot. If they make the run from west to east, we can travel along the back bearing and hopefully stumble over the drop. However, although there will be less margin for error, we are still going to need a major slice of luck if it isn't going to take us for ever to find the drop.'

'Won't the jet jockeys object to overflying an air-field?' Geordie said.

'I shouldn't think so. In strategic terms the area we're talking about is in the back of beyond; the last hostiles alert they had was probably when Alexander the Great was passing through, and anyway, they will be flying at zero feet at 600 knots in the middle of the night. If there are any potential hostiles on the ground, by the time they react, the Tornado will be long gone. If they think anything about it at all, they will probably tell themselves that it's one of their own aircraft on a secret mission and then roll over and go back to sleep.'

Shepherd and his mates hashed and re-hashed every option and every drawback imaginable until they had settled on what they thought was a workable plan. They then went on to draw up a wish list of the operational kit that they would need in the resupply.

'Right,' Shepherd said. 'First: comms. Jimbo?'

'Well, the first thing is that to save time we must have some low wattage, UHF radios. Those work on line of sight and if they have a low wattage output, then they have a limited range. It will be long enough for us to communicate with each other, but will make it very difficult for anyone else to intercept them, and they will save us a lot of time on the ground.'

'Okay. Agreed? Next: charges. Geordie?'

'We'll need a Packet Easy, with extra roles of det-cord. That will be far more standard charges and the associated switches, initiation sets, detonators, tape and fuses, than we are ever likely to use, but remember the old regimental maxim: If in doubt, take P for Plenty. It will have everything we need to take out a large target and lots to spare. And we'll need the extra det-cord in case we have to make large ring mains.'

'Some anti-tank mines would be handy too,' Jock said. 'Either the British Mark Sevens or the Russian T-46's. The Mark Sevens by choice because they pack a lot more punch than the Russian ones. I used one on the ranges once and it blew a tank hulk so far in the air, it disappeared over the horizon. And instead of the standard fuses, we want ratchet fuses. They can be set so that they will explode after however many vehicles we choose have run over the mine, rather than exploding when the first vehicle runs over it. Those cause panic in convoys because once the drivers have seen a couple of those go off, everybody gets the idea and nobody feels safe, even the ones at the very back of the column.'

'A couple of RPG-7's would be nice too,' Geordie said, 'just to give us a bit more firepower and punch.'

Shepherd nodded. 'And I'm sure there'll be a few more things to add to the shopping list before we're finished.'

'You can't beat enthusiasm,' Jock said, 'but just to inject another note of caution, Hereford is only one cog in this machine, and the others further up the food chain don't trust humint, especially when it comes from Trogs like us. They're going to take days to sanction this op and that's if they ever do get around to approving it at all. The only way I can see that we'll be sure of getting the go-ahead is if they find themselves between a rock and a hard place. My point is, if they do let us go ahead it will likely only be to stop the Israelis planning something similar and starting World War Three in the process.'

'Even allowing for the usual Caledonian gloom, you're probably right Jock,' Shepherd said, 'but we have to keep working on it. By the time we get the go-ahead – if we do – it will be too late then to start detailed planning. So we will have to assume we are going to go and that we will get a resupply, and plan accordingly.'

Jimbo carried out the laborious task of sending messages to the Head Shed using the one time pad. His messages received the same tedious, fence-sitting response of "Wait out". While Jimbo was deciphering messages, Shepherd and the others kept repeatedly pulling the plan apart and reassembling it until they were satisfied that, with a successful airdrop and a fair wind, they had a reasonable chance of success.

Even then, they still kept chewing away at the problem, continually dissecting, analysing and modifying the plan and looking for flaws in it.

Three days later Jimbo returned from wrestling with the antique comms equipment with a jubilant smile on his face. 'We've been given provisional clearance to go ahead ... up to a point. The Head Shed says we can move to the border but we are not to cross it until sanctioned to do so by them. We have to listen out on our receivers and they've given us the channel settings, the code words and the transmission times.'

They all clustered around the map as he spread it out in front of them. 'I've also got the track for the resupply aircraft, if it happens, and it's like you predicted, Spider. The beginning of the run will be from a small airfield here,' he said, tapping the map with his finger. 'It's little more than a grass strip apparently, so the chances of there being any serious air defence kit around it are pretty minimal.' He moved his finger across the map. 'And the end of the run will be a distinctive, V-shaped cleft in the ridge over here. From that we can work out a very rough line of march to find the drop.'

'Bloody hell,' Geordie said. 'Given the scale of this map, that's leaving us a lot of ground to cover. It'll be like trying to find a 5p piece on the Long Sands at Tynemouth.'

'And we know that's impossible,' Jock said. 'If word got out that there was five pence somewhere on the beach, we'd be trampled to death by the stampede of over-excited Geordies looking for the biggest payday they've had in years.'

'Bloody hell, now I've heard everything,' Geordie said. 'A Glaswegian calling someone else tight.'

'If you two have finished bickering,' Jimbo said. 'We've also been given three options on the airdrop, so we will get three, four or five days warning before the drop comes in. It sounds like they're keeping their options open and hoping they can find some other way of dealing with the problem. But, listen up, they've also told us that the wing tanks will have a limited shelf life. If we don't find them in time, they will self-destruct and even if we do get to them in time, we will still have to neutralise the booby-traps they've fitted to them to stop the Iranians picking them up and then showing them on TV as yet another example of Western aggression.'

Shepherd shrugged. 'Despite all the caveats, it's still great news, guys. At least we can now get moving, because this waiting around is always a killer. The race to get to the resupply is going to make the time-scale of our planning much tighter than we thought, but I guess we can deal with that on the ground. Oh, and I know that weight is going to be at a premium but we need some basic tools, as well. You never know, they might well come in handy later on.'

While the SAS men had been formulating their plans, Ahmad had rounded up five motorbikes from among his followers up and down the valley. They were old but in good working order and to make sure they would last the journey, he had got a couple of local mechanics and metalworkers to service them and make some modifications to Shepherd's specifications. They had fitted an additional plastic fuel tank above the existing tank on each bike and fixed brackets on either side of both wheels, holding a total of four jerry cans. On top of that each of the patrol members would carry another two jerry cans on a yoke around their body. 'At least it will be a quick death if a shot hits us,' Ahmad said.

'Only if the round goes right through both walls of the jerry can,' Shepherd said. 'It's very hard to set liquid fuel alight. So unless they're lucky enough to hit the mix of fuel vapour and air at the very top of the can. If a round does hit it, all that's likely to happen is that your legs will get drenched in petrol.'

'Well, all going well, we'll probably have enough fuel to make the return journey,' Ahmad said.

Shepherd shook his head. 'I doubt it. I suspect that we will be coming back another way.'

Chapter 13

They left the Panjshir Valley early the next morning, riding on the back of one of the many vividly painted trucks travelling the western arm of the Salang Highway towards Mazar-al-Sharif and Herat. Ahmad had flagged the truck down and persuaded the driver to accommodate them, though little persuasion was necessary – anyone travelling through the Panjshir Valley knew it was wise not to antagonise the followers of the great Ahmad Shah Massoud. Ahmad sat up front in the cab, squashed in with two of his cousins riding shotgun alongside the driver, while Shepherd and his team were in the back with their equipment, surrounded by rugs, pots and pans and the main cargo: a couple of hundreds sacks of potatoes.

The load had been re-stacked to leave a concealed space in the middle, large enough to hide the four SAS men, their motorbikes and weapons and the rest of their operational equipment. They would be visible from the air to anyone over-flying the truck, but that was a very unlikely scenario and they were well hidden from anyone one the ground or in another vehicle.

They were dressed as locals, their fair skin by now burned a ruddy brown by the wind and sun, once more with the exception of Jock, whose milk-bottle white or beetroot red skin – the only colours it ever went by natural means – had been dyed with fake tan to the colour of slightly orange mahogany. They wore loose brown Afghan garments covering their Western dress and the local woollen pakol hats that hid the colour of their hair. When they thought they might be seen, they kept scarves loosely wrapped around their faces. The only thing they could not hide was their eyes.

'That will not be a problem,' Ahmad had said when they raised that with him. 'There are plenty of Afghans and Iranians who are of Caucasian descent and have blue eyes. You can see them everywhere.' He laughed. 'And of course, they all claim to be descendants of Alexander the Great.'

They faced a marathon journey but made good progress at first, the road being mainly hardtop with the occasional graded stretch and less potholed than many of the other Afghan roads they had seen. For the most part, Shepherd and the others were able to ride on top of the cargo, enjoying the views, and they only climbed down into their hideaway when they were nearing towns or villages, where the truck might have to slow down or stop.

Things had been going smoothly when, many hours into the journey, but still an hour or so short of Islam Qala, the ramshackle town and smugglers' haven straddling the Afghani/Iranian border, they heard Ahmad shout 'Look out, trouble ahead!'

They ducked down into their hiding place at once, but looking through a gap in the sacks of potatoes and between the slats of the truck, Shepherd could see a group of about fifteen heavily armed men, drawn up in a semi-circle across the road ahead of them. Most of them were carrying AK-47s but a couple were pointing RPG 7's at the vehicle. They had also dragged boulders across the road, making it impossible to drive through without slowing to a crawl to negotiate the S-bend through the boulders.

Ahmad jumped down from the truck as soon as it had slowed to a stop and he and the leader of the gang at once launched into a verbal slanging match. While their leader was wrangling with Ahmad, the rest of the armed group grew more and more agitated and aggressive, gesticulating and pointing their weapons at the truck. One of the ambushers then cocked his AK-47 and put a round into one of the truck's front tyres which exploded with a bang. At this Ahmad's cousins jumped out of the cab brandishing their own weapons. There was a brief Mexican stand-off but, seeing their victims apparently so heavily outnumbered and outgunned, the ambushers' attitude and body-language made it clear that they were itching to turn it into a bloody shoot-out.

The tension was continuing to mount, both sides fingering their weapons, when a sack of potatoes suddenly tumbled from the back of the truck. It landed on the tarmac with a thud and split open, spilling potatoes in all directions. Surprised, the ambushers stared as the potatoes rolled around in the dirt, until one of them made a cracking sound, a handle flew off and smoke started to pour from it. The ambushers' expressions began to change as the realisation dawned that they were looking at a grenade, not a potato, but they still stood transfixed, apparently unable to move.

From the back of the truck they heard a quiet voice, speaking in a strong Glaswegian accent, saying, 'Five seconds. Stand by. Stand by.' As the grenade went off with a concussive blast, the voice shouted, 'GO!'

The SAS team vaulted to the ground on either side of the truck and, in classic Close Quarter Battle tactics, used controlled double-taps to take out the ambush group, firing and rolling to avoid presenting a target, shooting the closest ones first and then working outwards, so as to kill the furthest away last.

The sounds were deafening, with all four of the SAS men's weapons rattling off incessant controlled fire, while the rapidly dwindling band of surviving ambushers fired off automatic bursts in reply. Ricochets whined from the boulders blocking the road, and a few rounds from the ambushers punched holes in the bodywork of the truck. One starred the windscreen a few inches from the terrified driver's head, and another shot out the other front tyre. They were the only semi-accurate shots that the ambushers managed to get away in reply to the SAS men's fusillade. For the rest, their aim was wild, with rounds passing wide of the SAS men or flashing over their heads as they kept firing and rolling, constantly changing positions to throw off their enemies' aim.

One of the men holding RPG 7s was killed in the first burst of fire, the second brought his weapon to bear on the truck but even as he was pressing the trigger, two rounds smacked into his forehead and he was thrown backwards. The RPG round still launched with a thunder-crack sound but the fiery trail flashed high and wide of the truck and detonated on the rocky hillside well above them.

Like all Afghan men, the ambushers had practically been born with a rifle in their hands, but never before had they been exposed to the level of intense, viciously accurate fire that they were now being subjected to. The firefight was over in less than a minute – just four seconds per ambusher – with every one of them now lying dead, their blood staining the grey dust covering the road. It had been so clinically done that none of the SAS men had even had to do a magazine change. They got to their feet and flashed each other a thumbs-up.

Shepherd at once set Ahmad and his cousins to make sure that the ambushers were all dead and there was a fresh rattle of gunfire as they put a bullet into the brain of each prone figure. They collected the dead men's weapons and ammunition, loading them aboard the truck, and then dragged the bodies off the road, threw them down into the deep ditch at one side of it and then rolled the road-block boulders down on top of them, crushing them into the dirt. Finally, snapping a couple of branches from a thorn bush, Ahmad's men swept dust over the blood spills in the road.

As he dusted himself down, Shepherd nodded to Jock. 'Nice work there, if I may say so, a classic distraction ploy.'

Jock smiled. 'Works every time, doesn't it?'

'What did you use?'

'A Yank M-67, they make more noise than damage. The arguing and shouting didn't seem to be going anywhere useful, so I thought I'd solve the problem before the wrangling went on any longer.' He paused. 'But do you know what worries me? I've got a feeling that it wasn't a random ambush, and they might actually have been waiting for us.'

'You might well be right,' Shepherd said. He gestured at the driver who had climbed out of his cab and was staring disconsolately at his truck, 'Anyway, given that our friend only seems to have one spare tyre and it could be days before he gets another, maybe it's time we left the truck and started out across country.'

'Sure,' Jock said. 'It will be a lot easier for us to hide, we'll be more secure and we'll be less likely to run into another bunch of local hoods as we get closer to the border.'

Shepherd nodded. 'Okay, let's start unloading the kit.' Within ten minutes they were riding their motorbikes away from the road and up into the hills. Ahmad was still with them, but as they only had five bikes, his cousins had been left behind to make their own way back to the Panjshir Valley on foot, while the truck driver sat in his cab, praying that someone from whom he could buy a spare tyre would come along before another gang of robbers arrived to strip him and his truck of all his merchandise.

At first the SAS men made painfully slow progress. The border area was volatile, alive with activity from groups of local tribesmen blocking even the most minor tracks and manning look-outs on some of the hilltops and ridges. The bikes were hugely overloaded and they could barely make progress across the rough terrain, often having to backtrack to find an easier route around an obstacle or pause to dig out their bikes when they became bogged down in patches of soft sand.

Despite their orders from the Head Shed to remain on the Afghan side of the border until clearance had been given, they barely paused when they reached the point where they thought the border was. In any case, it was ill-defined and almost non-existent on the ground, just a few man-made stone cairns along the line of a high, rocky watershed. After consulting with his comrades, Shepherd had decided it was safer to go straight on into Iran than risk loitering close to the border.

'Nice to see you're respecting the CO's orders,' Jock said with a sardonic smile.

Shepherd grinned back at him. 'Why break the habit of a lifetime? In any case, what's the worst that can happen? If it all goes to rat-shit, or the Head Shed goes mental about it, we can always retrace our tracks and come out again.' He twisted the throttle and led the way on into Iran.

The terrain beyond the border was rough and hilly country, intersected by deep valleys that ran at right angles to their chosen course, forcing them into long detours or a wearying succession of climbs to the ridgelines, picking their way around cliffs and boulder fields, followed by rough, scree-strewn descents into the next valley. Avoiding the bridges, which were always well watched and guarded, they then had to find a way to ford the fast-rushing rivers in the valley floor, still swollen with meltwater from the winter snows, and then begin yet another steep ascent.

Travelling only by night and as far as possible keeping to animal tracks along the sides of the hills, they saw numerous picket fires on the ridge tops above them, but they were not challenged again, even though at times the noise of their motorbike engines must have been clearly audible to the local tribesmen. Unlike their kin on the Afghan side of the frontier, the Iranian border tribes seemed either too lazy, too poorly motivated or too disinterested to worry about five strangers inching their way through their territory on battered motorbikes.

'Perhaps they're looking for bigger game,' Geordie said, 'like vehicles carrying valuable cargo and attempting to beat the blockade.'

'They'd have to have quite some vehicles to beat the blockade across this terrain,' Jock said. 'I wouldn't fancy it in a farm tractor, let alone a truck.'

They kept to their normal routine: the Special Forces Standard Operating Procedure. They moved only by night, using passive night goggles to penetrate the darkness and then lay up to rest during the daylight hours. At daybreak they scattered over an area of a few kilometres, each selecting a lying up position so that they could see at least one of their comrades, then spent the day in fitful sleep, most of the time just watching and listening, using their binoculars to scan the ground. If they were not making any noise, they would hear anyone else in the area long before they got close to the patrol. If they were severely compromised they would use their RV procedures to escape and meet up again to continue the mission.

As they travelled further west, the terrain became flatter, drier and dustier, and the weather turned warmer. Their bikes trailed columns of dust behind them but once more, they appeared to arouse little alarm or interest in the people they glimpsed in the distance, tending their flocks or crops. Like their cousins in Afghanistan and Pakistan, the Iranian border tribes were invariably indifferent, if not downright hostile, to their governments. Most of them made at least part of their income through smuggling and had little reason to co-operate with the police and military forces who descended on them only to launch punitive raids, confiscate goods or exact bribes from them, and when government money was being spent very little of it ever seemed to trickle down to those living in the far-flung frontier provinces.

The SAS men travelled on, leaving the wild borderlands and passing through lush cultivated areas, fed by irrigation ditches sourced from dams higher up in the mountains. It was easy to avoid the few villages they saw and they were growing increasingly optimistic about their mission. Leaving the farmland behind, they next found themselves on a high, flat plain, with clumps of small thorny bushes interspersed among the gravel and coarse, gritty sand. The plain was criss-crossed with animal tracks but there was no sign of humans, yet in spite of this, Shepherd could not shake off a growing, uneasy feeling that they were being watched.

Resting in his lying up position several days into the journey, Jimbo was mildly surprised to hear on his radio the code-words authorising the go-ahead for the mission and the air drop. 'Bloody hell,' he said, as he discussed it with the others before setting off that night. 'I was fully expecting the mission to be aborted.'

'Just as well we didn't wait at the border like we were ordered,' Geordie said. 'If we had done, by the time we got the go-ahead, we would never have had enough time left to cover the distance to the target.'

'The Head Shed know us too well by now,' Shepherd said. 'I bet they never seriously expected us to wait at the border. They knew full well we'd just cross over and get on with it and that way, if we had been compromised, they would have covered their arses with their bosses up the line by claiming that they'd forbidden us to go ahead.'

They neither saw nor heard the Tornado making the resupply drop but they did hear some other occasional fast jet air activity in the distance which they assumed was the Iranian response to the air incursion by the Tornado. 'Bit late now, stable door and all that,' Geordie said with a laugh.

'At least it looks as if the air-drop has been made,' said Shepherd. 'I just hope it doesn't turn into a needle and haystack situation.'

They now began an intensely frustrating time trying to locate the resupply. They had found the easternmost datum point without too much difficulty, but there was too large a margin of error when making calculations using their crude, large-scale escape map. That lack of precision forced them to travel in line abreast across the plain, and they had to pause and detour to look into every small dip and fissure large enough to hide a fast jet's fuel tank.

'It's not just the mapping we've got to work with,' Jock said. 'We've become less skilled in the basics and too dependent on GPS.'

'Hark at Granddad,' Geordie said. 'Everything was so much better in your day, wasn't it? At least you didn't need petrol for the old horse and cart.'

Although he maintained an optimistic front, Shepherd was privately beginning to despair of ever finding the resupply. They were still widely separated, line abreast, as they travelled across the plain, and they stayed isolated from each other when lying up through the day, each finding their own place – a thorn bush, a group of boulders, a dip in the ground – in which to remain hidden while they communicated with each other by hand signals.

They had spent the night in another vain attempt to find the air drop and before dawn, as usual, the team had split up to find secure lying up places. Shepherd had found a clump of thorn bushes large enough to hide his bike and himself. He had used the pair of folding secateurs, which every Special Forces soldier carried as a matter of routine, to work his way deep into the clump. He cut the stems close to the ground, opening up a way into the heart of the thorn bushes and then replaced them behind him, obscuring him from sight. The branches would wither and die in a few days but by then Shepherd would be long gone.

He had cat-napped for a few hours when he found himself instantly wide awake. Something had triggered his alert but as yet he did not know what it was. Even with his eyes closed, the angle of the fierce sunlight filtering through the thorny branches onto his face told him it was late morning. His right hand rested reassuringly on his Kalashnikov rifle while, with every sense at full alert, he tried to identify what had brought him back to consciousness.

Keeping his eyes lightly shut, he used his hearing and sense of smell to try to pin down the source of his disquiet. He kept his head resting on his belt kit which he was using as a pillow while he came to terms with the situation. He had been asleep a few moments before but he remembered exactly where he was, in Iran, somewhere south-east of Tehran. He knew he was lying in the middle of a thorn bush. There was still no noise, movement or scent on the breeze to explain his alertness, but he sensed someone watching him, a pair of eyes focused intently on his face, willing him to wake up.

He slowly opened his eyes and was momentarily dazzled by the sunlight, but as his vision cleared, he found himself confronted by the smiling face of a young lad about twelve years old.

'Hello sir,' the boy said in almost accentless English.

'Hello,' said Shepherd, wondering, despite himself, if he was really still asleep and dreaming. 'Who are you?'

The boy grinned. 'My name is Boy. What is your name?'

'Dan' said Shepherd, sitting up. 'How come you speak English?

'I am taught by my grandfather and we listen to the BBC World Service every day.'

'I see. Now, is this just a social call or can I help you in some way?' Shepherd said, amused that here in the middle of an Iranian desert, the two of them were conversing like a pair of little old ladies in a Home Counties tea room.

'Could you please come with me to meet my grandfather? He has asked me to come and fetch you.'

Shepherd made a quick mental run through of all the options available to him, and decided that, for the moment, the only viable one was to do as the lad wanted. They could not afford to have the boy or his grandfather going off and reporting them to the authorities so the safest option was to go with the flow for the moment. He first made a quick hand signal to Jock and the rest of the team. Unfortunately no system of hand signals had ever been devised that could express 'I've been discovered by a local lad, but I don't think we are compromised yet. Wait out and I'll see what the story is.' Instead he had to content himself with the one that meant 'going for a recce', and then crawled out from under the thorn bushes. 'So where is your grandfather?' asked Shepherd.

'I will take you to him,' the boy said. 'Don't worry, it isn't far.'

True to his word, the boy had only taken him a few hundred yards before Shepherd saw an agitated group of people sitting in a fold in the ground. They were so well hidden and well camouflaged, wearing robes that perfectly matched the colours of the terrain in which they lived, that they would have been all but invisible to anyone from even a few feet away. In the centre of the group was an elderly man with a face as wrinkled and brown as a nut. On seeing Shepherd approaching, his face lit up and he stood up and held out his hand.

'I'm truly sorry to bother you, old chap, but we have a problem which we think you may be able to help us with,' he said, as Shepherd did a second double-take at the flawless Oxford English emanating from the mouth of a nomadic Iranian tribesman.

'I'm sorry but I have to ask, how come you speak such good English?' asked Shepherd.

The old man smiled. 'Many years ago, in the days of the Shah, I worked for the Anglo Iranian Oil Company near the Shatt al Arab river. I had begun as a houseboy but the company then retrained me to become a school teacher. The British were always very honourable, I still receive a pension every year from them, although my son now has to go to a bank in Bahrain to collect it. I am now teaching my grandson English – it is the language of gentlemen and the language of the future – in the hope that he too will be able to go and work for a British company somewhere in the Gulf.' He paused and held Shepherd's gaze. 'However, much more important for now, is that fact that four of our young boys have been kidnapped by the troops of a bastard called Colonel Farehdi. If they are not freed, I shudder to think what will happen to them. We cannot free them – we don't have the manpower or the weaponry – but we have been watching you and your friends, and we think that, perhaps with the aid of the bombs you have been searching for, you may be able to do it for us.'

Shepherd gave a rueful smile, though his ears had pricked up at the mention of "bombs". 'I thought we were good,' he said, 'but we could certainly learn something from you. I had an uneasy feeling of being watched for a few days now but I never saw as much as a trace of you.'

The old man made a gesture with his hand, as if brushing the compliment away. 'You do not know this country as we do and we have long experience in avoiding trouble. There are many people – smugglers, warlords, rustlers, thieves – who wish us ill and the government and the army-' He paused and spat into the dust. 'They have never trusted nomads like us. They want to take us off our lands, fence in our flocks and ourselves so that we become good, obedient citizens, but that is not our way. We live the life our ancestors have led for countless generations and we shall not change those ways to please any Ayatollah, Shah, or any other tyrant – Iranian or foreign – who tries to force us. We have indeed been watching you and your fellows, and normally we would have let you pass through our lands without interference, but I'm afraid that we are desperate. The boys had been out looking for some lost animals when the army patrol stumbled across them.' He spread his hands in a helpless gesture. 'We have warned them again and again, but boys will be boys, and do not always listen to their elders.' He ruffled the boy's hair as he was saying it. 'They grew careless and were captured. The soldiers have taken them back to their camp but luckily one of the boys was able to wriggle free and he ran off. Those soldiers...' Again he paused and spat in the sand, '–were too soft and lazy to pursue him far into the desert and when they gave up the chase, he was able to get back to us and tell us what had happened. As I said, there are too many soldiers and they are too well-armed for us to fight them, but it is imperative that the boys are rescued before Farehdi himself gets his hands on them.'

Shepherd's immediate instinct was to help the old man, but he was very conscious too that any time spent on that task would leave even less time to fulfil their main mission. Sensing his indecision, the old man clinched the deal by saying, 'If you help us to free our boys, we will take you to the place where your bombs are hidden.'

'You've really found them?' Shepherd said.

He nodded. 'We saw them fall. Don't worry, they are quite safe, and no one but us knows where they are.'

Shepherd thought for only a moment longer, then said 'All right. I need to talk to my colleagues first, but I will try to help you.'

One of the nomads, holding what looked like an ancient Martini-Henry hunting rifle that appeared to be a century or more old, escorted Shepherd back across the desert to where his team were lying up. The man stood to one side, aloof but watchful, while he put them in the picture. 'I'll have to do it,' Shepherd said.

'We are not here to carry out some humanitarian mission,' Jock said.

'I'm well aware of that, but we need that resupply for the mission we are here for, and I get the feeling that we could search from now till doomsday and still not find the site of the air-drop, whereas the old man says he can lead us straight to it.'

'We could force him to tell us,' said Jock.

Shepherd shook his head. 'Hearts and minds, Jock. Remember?'

'It's still a risk,' Geordie said.

'I know, but it's one I'll just have to take,' said Shepherd. 'You guys remain in cover. If I don't make it back, the old man has promised that he will guide you to the resup and you will then still have a good chance of completing the mission.'

Before there could be any further argument about it, he turned on his heel and walked away, with his guide leading him back to the nomads' temporary camp in the fold in the ground.

CHAPTER 14

Guided by the boy, Shepherd set off at once to OP the army camp where the other boys were being held prisoner. The boy led him for miles across the desert and Shepherd had time to marvel at his tradecraft. The terrain was virtually featureless, a sand and gravel plain studded with thorny scrub and with few high points or ridges, but the boy steered an unerring course, never hesitating for a moment.

At last, as they made their way up a low incline, the boy paused and then whispered, 'We are very close now.' He dropped to the ground and began to belly-crawl forward. Shepherd followed his example and within a couple of minutes he was hidden from sight in a shallow dip in the ground, looking out over a fly-blown army camp, a few hundred yards away.

The heat was fierce as the sun reached its zenith and the strengthening wind blew stinging flurries of sand at them, forcing Shepherd to tighten the scarf around his face, but these were minor discomforts. He took only occasional small sips from his water bottle, conserving his supplies, and he spent most of the rest of the day just observing the camp and the soldiers' routines. They were downwind of the camp and could easily hear the troops shouting to each other as they struggled to keep themselves comfortable. There were six Russian yurt-style tents, but they were sagging against the increasingly strong wind, with the guy ropes slack and the tent pegs loose in the ground. A tattered marquee-style tent stood forlornly in the centre of the compound. Nearby were two ex-Soviet BTR-60 PB armoured personnel carriers, eight-wheeled monsters with steel plating strong enough to stop a 7.62 mm round and a gun turret housing a heavy machine gun whose rounds could penetrate armour plate at 500 metres range. 'They look like monsters,' the boy whispered.

Shepherd smiled. 'I can see where you're coming from,' he said. 'The sloping snout and the raised shutters over the twin windscreens, do make it look a bit like some mythical creature's face, don't they?'

The armoured personnel carriers were parked untidily, alongside an ancient, battered Zil-130 truck, still in its factory blue paint though it was sun-faded and the metal was showing through in places where the paint had flaked. It was hitched to a four-wheeled water bowser and next to that was a mobile field kitchen, with smoke drifting up from the chimney and steam rising from the boiler. Close by a small herd of fat little goats, bleating pitifully, were tethered to a metal stake.

'The thieving bastards,' Boy muttered in his impeccable English accent. 'Those are our fucking goats.' Shepherd gave him a sideways look.

'Where did you learn to swear like that?'

The lad shrugged but didn't answer.

On the far side of the compound, in contrast to the shabbiness of the rest of the camp, Shepherd could see an immaculate, olive green tent of US or British Army design. It was flanked by a hessian-screened, improvised shower and toilet area. Everything in that part of the camp looked pristine, making Shepherd almost certain that it was where the Iranian officer was based but he could see no sign of life from the tent and no trace of the officer elsewhere in the camp.

The whole of the camp was surrounded by a single coil of concertina razor wire, with only a vehicle entrance, guarded by two tired, dust-covered sentries, to one side, and an unguarded walkway through on the opposite side. All the time Shepherd and the boy were watching, no vehicles had entered or left but there were scores of vehicle tracks across the desert, showing up clearly where the crust of the plain had been broken, exposing the light coloured sand underneath.

Occasionally, a soldier emerged from one of the yurts, paused to pick up a tin of water and then wandered off through the gap in the wire, heading into the desert, before squatting down in the sand. The lack of any trench latrines and defensive trenches, not to mention the lack of camp discipline, suggested the camp was a very short-term deployment.

'I bet there's a lot of Egyptian PT going on over there as well,' Shepherd said.

The boy gave him a puzzled look. 'What?'

'It's an old British Army joke: it means they're spending a lot of time sleeping.'

Boy frowned. 'The joke is that Egyptian people are lazy?'

'I guess so.'

The lad nodded solemnly. 'I did not know that.'

Shepherd calculated the troop strength in the camp at about platoon-strength: twenty-five men. He based this on each of the armoured personnel carriers holding eight fighting troops and a crew of two, plus odds and sods like cooks and guards. Normally a platoon would have been commanded by a lieutenant, but judging by the lay-out and quality of the officer's accommodation, Shepherd surmised it was occupied by someone of higher rank. As he kept watch, he was easily able to identify the weapons carried by the troops as G3's, designed by Heckler and Koch, but manufactured under licence in Iran. Old but reliable, those rifles fired the standard Nato 7.62 round. If one of those rounds hit you, you stayed hit.

Shepherd kept his gaze moving over the camp area, scanning it through his stabilised binoculars, but he could have kicked himself when, after already having observed the camp for a couple of hours, he suddenly spotted another sentry that he had not noticed before, stationed outside one of the yurts. He could only have missed him earlier because the sentry had been out of sight on the other side of the tent, but Shepherd spotted him because he had moved to stretch his legs. 'That answers the most important question of all,' he said to the boy, 'where the prisoners are being held.'

'My friends?' asked Boy.

'Exactly,' said Shepherd.

Occasionally a tough looking NCO would stick his head into the entrance to one of the yurts and ball out the troops inside it. That invariably led to a Laurel and Hardy type scene when, in their frantic anxiety to do the NCO's bidding, the soldiers would come scrambling from the tent, colliding with each other, dropping their weapons and falling over in their haste to pacify him until, to their visible relief, the NCO was satisfied and stomped off, allowing them to disappear back into their tent.

Having studied the lay-out of the camp and the routines of the guards, and noted the general air of incompetence of the soldiers, Shepherd developed his plan, then outlined it to the boy and explained his part in it. 'Don't forget to run away when I get close to the sentry,' he said at the end of the briefing. 'I don't want to have to come back and rescue you afterwards. And Boy? If I don't get back, take my kit to my friend Jock who you have been watching, and tell him what happened.'

'I promise I will, sir,' the boy said, his face suddenly looking much older than his years.

Just before dusk they saw a Russian jeep, a soft-topped UAZ-469, approach the compound at high speed, trailing a cloud of dust behind it. It was still in its Soviet army green livery, which made it visible for miles against the background of the arid, sandy plain. The sentries saluted clumsily as the jeep swept past them into the compound and drove across it to the officer's tent before slewing to a halt. The jeep driver quickly jumped out and dashed to open the passenger door, helping his passenger out of the vehicle, then saluted smartly and waited until the officer entered the tent before moving off towards the field kitchen.

Watching intently through his binoculars, Shepherd saw that the jeep had a pennant fluttering from its bonnet, and its seats had pristine looking white covers on them. As the officer stood in the entrance to the tent looking out, Shepherd was able to bring him into close-up with the binoculars. He saw that he was wearing the insignia of a colonel and was a short, overweight man, clean shaven with an oily sheen on his face, and dressed incongruously in a clean and pressed dark brown uniform, complemented by a British-style Sam Browne belt, complete with pistol holster and swagger stick. Even through his binoculars Shepherd could see the cruel twist to the man's face as he stared balefully at his men before walking off towards the camp kitchen. 'This must be the infamous Colonel Farehdi,' he said, to himself as much as to the boy. 'He's a cunning bastard.

He doesn't go far from his vehicle because that's his escape ticket if anything goes wrong.'

The sun was now sinking towards the western horizon and the fierce heat of the day was beginning to dissipate. 'Okay, it's almost time for action,' he said to the boy. 'Remember what I told you.' He indicated his weapon and belt kit. 'Stick to the plan and get that to Jock. And Boy?' He undid his shirt and fished around his waist. 'This is for you.' He handed the boy a leather money belt worn shiny from his sweat and from rubbing against his skin.

'It contains five Tola gold bars, and each bar weighs about fifty-five grams, so there's over a quarter of a kilo in weight altogether. The gold is ninety-nine percent pure and the hallmarks are recognised everywhere and have been since the time of the East India Company. It's yours to keep whether I get back or not.' He paused, clocking the boy's half-excited, half-sceptical expression. 'Don't worry, it really is gold and I promise you that it's not been stolen. It's what we soldiers call blood money, to be used to buy my way out of a life or death situation. Well, you saved me, so I'm giving it to you. You'll be able to trade it in any souq for enough money to pay your way through university when you grow up. I'd recommend trying the United Arab Emirates, I'm told the universities there are excellent. Okay?'

The boy had unzipped the belt a little, revealing the glint of gold inside and, barely able to tear his gaze away from it, he began to stammer his thanks.

'Forget about it,' Shepherd said. 'Like I said, you've earned it.' He grinned. 'Or at least you will have done by the time you've got me down to the entrance of that camp. Just give me a moment to get ready.'

While the boy knotted the belt around his own waist, under his robes, Shepherd stripped off the scarf wrapped around his head and his outer layer of local clothing, revealing his hair colour and the military shirt and combat fatigues he'd been wearing beneath the local clothes. Then he lay down and began to roll around in the dirt, coating his face and hair, the inside of his nostrils and the inside of his mouth with dust, until he looked like someone who had been lost in the desert for days. With his shirt unbuttoned and hanging open, exposing his chest and abdomen, he looked thin to the point of emaciation. Only the keenest eye would have noted the still phenomenal tone and condition of his lean body.

When he left Hereford he had been seven to ten pounds overweight, having deliberately over-eaten so that he was carrying some excess fat. He had guessed that this operation was going to be an exceptionally hard one, operating in a region where it was going to be very unlikely that he'd be able to find the food necessary to replace the 7,500 or more calories a day his body would be burning. So, like the other members of the patrol, he deliberately "ate for Britain" before the op began, relying on his body to feed on itself when other food was in short supply. He knew he would gradually lose the excess poundage but had hoped to be back home before his body started to eat into his muscular tissue. However, he had miscalculated, and knew he needed R & R and a chance to build up his bodily reserves again soon.

Now smothered in dust from head to foot, he made his final preparations, loosening the flexi-saw around his waist so he could withdraw it quickly if needed, and palming the knife blade from his boot sole, taking a calculated gamble that he would be given only a perfunctory search before the action began. Taking a deep breath he left his cover and, with the boy alongside him, began to move towards the camp.

CHAPTER 15

As night was approaching, the two sentries on the gate had instinctively drawn closer together. They were simple souls, conscripted from the other side of Iran and they felt scared and isolated. Their unease was heightened by Colonel Farehdi, the monster who was constantly upbraiding and abusing them, terrifying them with bloodcurdling tales of foreign mercenaries coming to get them if they didn't stay alert. Suddenly, one of the men had his worst fears realised. He could see and hear an apparition approaching out of the desert, a stumbling, white-faced creature, supported by a boy shouting in Farsi for help. 'Save him! Save him! He's dying! He needs help!' He could see the apparition was wearing a military uniform and he knew it was not an Iranian one. He turned to tell his fellow-guard to watch them while he went for help, only to realise that his comrade had already run screaming into the camp.

The sentry was from the far south of Iran where djinns and spirits were known to exist and to roam the land at night. When he plucked up the courage to look up again, the dust-covered ghost was lying in the dirt at his feet and the boy had vanished into the night.

Through half-closed eyes, feigning unconsciousness, Shepherd watched the situation develop. He could see the first sentry running through the camp gate, shouting and waving his arms, and the other one backing away from him, fear written all over his face, still with his Heckler and Koch G3 slung over his shoulder. In his panic, the man appeared to have forgotten that he was armed. A couple of minutes later, a mob of soldiers came running back through the gates, some half-dressed, others half-asleep, and headed by a very angry sergeant. The NCO peered at Shepherd's recumbent body and then rounded on the troops, lashing out, kicking and shouting orders at them, until at last several of them pounced on Shepherd, lifted him up and carried him bodily into the camp.

They carted him into the mess tent, dimly lit by a couple of paraffin pressure lamps, and then dumped him on the dirt floor. By now in an uncontrollable rage, the sergeant began kicking Shepherd unmercifully about the head and body. Shepherd made no attempt to ward off or cushion the blows; he wanted them to believe he was unconscious.

Thankfully the beating lasted only a few seconds before there was a shout from the doorway. The group parted and from under his eyelids, Shepherd glimpsed the figure of Colonel Farehdi striding in, still in his dress uniform, complete with Sam Browne belt and swagger stick. On his barked command, the troops fell upon Shepherd again and lifted him up onto the mess table. He shouted another command and they removed his boots and socks, fumbling with them clumsily in their desperate eagerness to please the officer who was feared and hated in equal measure.

Many eager hands pinned Shepherd to the table as Farehdi pulled his bamboo swagger stick from his belt and began lashing the soles of Shepherd's feet until he was red in the face and totally out of breath. The pain was agonising but Shepherd gritted his teeth and held himself still, head lolling to one side as if too far gone to know or care what was being done to him.

'Who are you?' asked Farehdi.

'I demand you treat me as a prisoner of war,' said Shepherd.

'There is no war here, my friend,' said Farehdi. 'And no Geneva Convention. That was just a taste of what is in store for you. There will be more when I have showered and eaten, and before I have finished with you, you will regret ever being born.' With another curt order to his men, Farehdi strode out again, leaving Shepherd surrounded by the still apprehensive crowd of soldiers. The sergeant, apparently unable to help himself, started to beat Shepherd around the head again. When he had finished, he turned his back on the prisoner and began to lecture the troops about the English mercenary scum that they had captured.

Even with his vision still impaired by the involuntary tears of pain in his eyes, Shepherd reacted instantly. He swivelled on his hands, snaked one bare foot under the sergeant's chin as the other clamped onto the back of his neck. With a savage push-pull motion, Shepherd broke the NCO's neck with an audible crack. He held him upright with his feet long enough to grab the man's weapon, then let the lifeless corpse drop to the ground.

The whole thing had taken less than a second, but it was more than enough to cause a fresh wholesale panic in the ranks. The conscripted rabble of troops might well never have fired a weapon in anger, nor seen someone killed before, least of all so close in front of them that they had heard his neck snap and the gasp and gurgle of his dying breath. As one man, forgetting whatever military discipline they might once have had, they made a mad scramble for the exit, partially demolishing the tent in their blind panic to get away.

To speed them on their way, Shepherd jumped down from the mess table and fired a couple of rounds from the sergeant's rifle in the general direction of the fleeing mob, then hurried across to the rear of the tent and used his knife blade to slit the canvas. He slipped through it and making little effort at concealment, made his way to the tent where he had spotted the sentry. Being without his boots was no handicap to him, for he had spent years going without footwear and hardening his feet with surgical spirit so that the skin was as hard as the soles of his boots.

It was now completely dark, the desert night having fallen like a cloak, with the only light coming from the millions of stars in the night sky. From the direction of the fleeing soldiers there were a few sporadic bursts of rifle fire, but they were so hasty and poorly aimed that the rounds passed well clear of Shepherd. He knew he had to move quickly if he wanted to get his revenge on Colonel Farehdi, but first he had to release the captive boys from the tribe and make sure they got away to safety. As he rounded the side of the tent where they were being held, the sentry, still standing in front of the entrance but obviously frightened by the shooting, was in a classic sentry pose, his rifle pointing towards Shepherd in the "on guard" position. It did him little good. Without even breaking stride, Shepherd downed the startled sentry with a blow from the butt of his rifle. He then relieved the unconscious soldier of all of his fully charged rifle magazines, stowing them around his pockets.

Throwing open the tent flap, Shepherd glanced inside and saw the four boys cowering on the sand in the farthest corner of the tent. Even in the dim light, he could clearly see that they had suffered at the hands of Farehdi and his soldiers, for their faces were bruised and blood-stained, and gaunt with fear. Shepherd tried to speak calmly and slowly, knowing that if he shouted he would spook the boys. He was unsure if any of them spoke English, so he also used sign language to indicate that they should come with him.

Slowly and very reluctantly, probably expecting to be shot as soon as they emerged from the tent, they followed him outside. They nudged each other as they saw the guard lying unconscious, blood seeping from his face and then followed Shepherd with slightly less reluctance as he led them to the camp gate.

At the gate he fired a quick burst in the general direction of the Iranian soldiers to keep their heads down, then urged the boys in the general direction of the place where the rest of their tribe were waiting for them. Still tentative at first, with more than a few anxious glances behind them, they began walking off into the desert, but gradually started moving faster and faster until at last they were running flat out, as quickly as they could in their weakened state.

Bursts of wild gunfire were still coming from the soldiers and Shepherd could see the flashes from the gun muzzles as the troops slowly began advancing back towards the camp. Taking up a firing position on top of one of the armoured personnel carriers, he put down a short barrage of withering fire towards the muzzle flashes. Almost immediately the firing wavered and the troops stopped their advance and dropped into cover.

Just as Shepherd was on the point of moving towards Farehdi's tent, he heard the UAZ jeep fire up. There was the grinding of gears and then the engine was over-revved, spinning the wheels and throwing up a fog of sand and dust, but then the tyres gripped and the jeep lurched forward, swerved through the camp gates and tore off, hell for leather, across the desert. It disappeared into the darkness with just the occasional flash of its brake lights showing the direction it was taking and they grew steadily dimmer the farther it travelled.

Shepherd was furious, both at Farehdi and himself, and in his anger fired a long burst in the general direction of the jeep, even though he knew it was pointless because the Iranian officer was already out of effective range. As he controlled his anger, he gave a rueful smile and metaphorically tipped his cap to Farehdi; the guy was certainly a survivor, but with luck that would not be the case after the next time they came face to face.

With the other Iranians still lying up in cover, waiting to be told what to do, Shepherd slipped out of the camp and began to make his way back to where he had earlier cached his kit. When he got there he was further annoyed to discover that there was no sign of the boy. He was on the point of heading back into the camp once more to look for him, when he heard the sound of somebody moving quickly across the desert towards him. He brought his AK to bear, but then lowered the barrel a moment later as he saw the boy approaching at a run, very out of breath.

'I'm sorry sir,' he said, as soon as he had got his breath back. 'But I had to go and release the goats, they are ours, not the soldiers. Now they will find their own way home to my people. Oh, and I brought your boots as well. You forgot them.' He held up the boots and Shepherd took them.

'For goodness sake Boy,' Shepherd said, 'you could've got yourself killed' but then he broke off and instead of carrying on with the bollocking, he burst out laughing instead. 'You've got some cool nerve there, Boy, I'll give you that. Maybe we'd better rethink the whole university thing, I'm not sure they'll be ready for someone like you!'

Shepherd sat down on the ground and pulled on his boots. Before they moved off, Shepherd checked the camp through his binoculars, making doubly sure that the soldiers were not preparing a patrol to pursue them. However, the troops he could see, though now back inside the camp, were huddled together around a fire, staring nervously out into the darkness and they clearly had no appetite at all for further skirmishes with him, especially as their NCO was dead and their commanding officer had fled.

CHAPTER 16

It took Shepherd and the boy just a few hours to get back to where the tribe was waiting for them. The four captives and the goats had already returned ahead of them and the sight of his grandson safe and well caused the boy's grandfather to dance a little jig in the sand and then crush Shepherd in an embrace. The nomads took him back across the desert to his patrol where the grateful tribe slaughtered a goat in celebration, fed them all and then kept watch while they snatched a few hours sleep. Before first light the next morning they led them to the site of the air-drop, a bowl-shaped depression about a kilometre across. It had proved to be no great distance at all from where the tribe had set up their camp, and Shepherd was annoyed with himself that they had not found the Tornado wing-pods under their own steam, though he was also grateful to the nomads for being true to their word.

Shepherd, Ahmad and the others squatted down on their haunches, quizzically examining the two fuel tank resupply pods. Their bikes and the rest of their kit were close by and there was a tangible feeling of expectation in the air. It was easy to see where the pods had hit the ground and then bounced, causing short sandy, scars on the desert floor. The drogue chutes which had slowed the tanks down and stopped them from being destroyed on impact, were now lying limp, draped over the nearby thorn bushes. While Shepherd's patrol began examining the pods, the nomads started to gather the chutes. 'We can make many things from this fabric,' the old man said.

The pods had a few scratches and minor dents on their metal skins but were otherwise undamaged. However, the immediate problem occupying the team was that every time they tried to approach the pods, a high pitched beeping sound began emanating from them, and if any of them got really close to the pods, the beeps gave way to the wail of a siren. They had already tested this several times and were now in the process of debating how to get around the problem.

In the vastness of the desert, the noise that the alarms gave off was no great cause for concern, especially as the nomads had posted look-outs to warn of any enemy approach, but the SAS men were undecided whether the alarms were all that was protecting the pods, or whether other, more dangerous security devices had also been fitted to them.

'They told us that the resupply would be booby-trapped,' Jock said, 'so I reckon that these are nothing more than warnings to scare off any local tribespeople who might have stumbled across them.'

Jimbo nodded. 'They'll have fitted proximity sensors to start beeping when anyone approaches, that's all.'

'Maybe so,' Shepherd said, 'but if you start tampering with them without disarming the devices first, my guess is that they are also going to go bang, big time. I've had a good look at the pods and I can't see anything on the surface at all, so I'm now going to take another look at the blunt end just to see if there is anything in the recess where the drogue chutes were stowed before they deployed. So everybody else stay here and I'll go forward on my own, just in case.'

Shepherd moved cautiously towards the back of the first pod, ignoring the beeping and then the high-pitched wail of the siren as he got closer to it. By lying prone on the ground and clearing away a small mound of sand that had been thrown up around it as it ploughed into the desert, he could just make out a small keypad with a roughly stencilled message alongside: "INSERT S OPERATIONAL NUMBER", inside the cavity where the drogue chute had been stowed. He breathed a huge sigh of relief because not only did this confirm that it was indeed their resupply, but it also revealed the code they needed to use to get at the contents. Every Special Forces soldier going on operations was allocated a unique three-digit number by which they were referred to in any communications. It was quicker to use a number in transmissions than a name, but more importantly, it protected the identity of the individual. "S" stood for Shepherd, so all that was needed was to enter his own number.

Shepherd quickly tapped in his three-digit code and the wailing siren immediately tailed away into silence. He waved for Jock to join him and they made their way to the second pod, and repeated the process, except that this time it was asking for Jock's Ops number. Having entered that, they set about opening the two resupply pods but it proved to be a slow and very laborious process. The pods had been sealed with a combination of adhesive and nuts and bolts, and although they had the tools that Shepherd had told them to bring with them from the Panjshir as part of their kit, opening the pods proved to be wearisomely time consuming for the impatient patrol.

'Right guys,' Shepherd said. 'First, we need to question the boy until we've got every bit of knowledge from him that we want, and once we've done that, he and his tribe can all scatter to the four winds. We don't want them anywhere near here in case things go wrong, because the Iranians will then use them as scapegoats and wipe them out. Once they're safely out of the way, we need to carry out target recces on the main site, plus any support sites, the military defences and the routes to and from them. We also must prepare this area for any follow-up by Farehdi and his troops. Let's start with the boy, then we can unpack the resupply and once we know what ordnance we have, we can allocate people to tasks. OK, let's get to it.'

They spent a considerable time pumping the boy dry, but most of what he knew was geographical, and he had not been too close to the target area for fear of being arrested. He offered to act as a guide but this was declined immediately by Shepherd as being too dangerous for the boy's people. Once they were happy that the nomads could be of no further help, Shepherd advised them to move on for their own safety.

There were prolonged farewells, in which the boy and his grandfather both touched their hands to their hearts in the traditional gesture as they said their own goodbyes. 'Manda nabashen, it means "may you keep your strength",' the grandfather said. Ahmad replied in Farsi, 'Zenda bashen – long life to you.' The boy had a tear in his eye when he turned away for the last time and the nomads began to move off across the desert. Within a few minutes they had disappeared as if they had been swallowed up by the earth.

'How the hell do they do that?' Jimbo said, scratching his head as he looked up and found the desert apparently empty of people, though they could see for at least a couple of miles in every direction.

What followed, once they had succeeded in opening the pods, was to test Shepherd's patience yet again. The contents of the resupply had been packed into the fuel tanks using expanding household foam.

189

Although it was an excellent cushioning material, it proved to be extremely difficult to remove. Each piece of equipment had to be carefully extracted from the foam using their sharp knives, while being very careful not to damage any of the weapons, radios or explosives that were enclosed. It took the best part of an hour to unpack the two tanks.

The contents had been coated in grease to preserve them from damp and condensation, but thankfully someone had also had the foresight to include a bottle of solvent and some rags to make the job of removing it much easier. Eventually, all of the contents had been unpacked, cleaned and laid out for an inventory check against the enclosed manifest list. Ahmad frowned when he saw the large box of condoms among the equipment.

'Notice that all of this kit is deniable,' Shepherd said. 'Most of it is ex-Soviet equipment and it is also either out of date, captured or taken from old stockpiles. If the Iranians do manage to get their hands on any of it, they won't be able to have a trial by television about who supplied it, because it could have come from anywhere in the world, including Iran itself. Even the fuel tanks they've used as the pods are from old F4s, which the Iranians are still flying, but they've been modified just enough to fit the Tornado. Someone has been very clever.' He stood up and stretched. 'Right, let's review the mission objectives. Although the destruction of the suspected nuclear facility or whatever else it is, remains the number one priority, the killing of Colonel Farehdi is next on the agenda.' He gave a bleak smile. 'You won't be the only one taking pleasure in seeing that achieved, Ahmad, and what we've already learned about him may well be the key to doing so. Like we said to you a while back: "Know Your Enemy", because if you do know the way he thinks and the way he is likely to react, you can force him or persuade him to take a course of action that you can then exploit to your advantage. That's what I'm hoping we can do in the final phases of the mission. Meanwhile, your task is to target recce the primary target. You should be able to gain entrance into the site without risking capture. It is a major project, so as well as a heavy military presence, there will be a very large civilian workforce and an awful lot of traffic in and out of the site. So if you look like an unthreatening local, either already working there, or hoping for a job, the chances are you won't even be challenged. If you are, just stick to your cover story. You're a builder or a labourer, or whatever, looking for work. They're not likely to make you demonstrate your building skills, or certainly not at the main gates anyway.'

Ahmad nodded.

'While he's doing that, Jock, you recce the military defences around the target, plus any other targets of opportunity,' Shepherd continued. 'Geordie, you take the recce of the area of the military camp, identify the type of vehicles being used by the guard force, and specifically whether they are tracked or wheeled, and if at all possible, try to identify the UAZ Jeep belonging to Farehdi himself. Jimbo, you and I will get busy preparing the area around the resupply drop zone as a killing ground for any follow-up action. And now that we all have transceiver radios, even though they're just short range UHF hand-held sets with a very limited range, things should be greatly speeded up. Everyone happy? Any Questions?' He was faced with shaking heads. 'Right then, let's get to it.'

The recce party left that night, with Jock and Geordie riding on two of the motorcycles, but with Ahmad on foot, walking far enough ahead of them to act as their eyes and ears, and keep a look-out for any Iranian army patrols or roadblocks, so that the two SAS men would not be taken by surprise.

They reached the target area and then ate some rations as they agreed an RV plan and a timetable to complete their tasks before splitting up. 'Right,' Shepherd said. 'This will be the first RV. Emergency RV here.' He jabbed the map with his finger. 'And War RV here. Any questions?' More shaking heads. 'Then good luck and, if I don't see you in hell, I'll see you in Hereford.'

CHAPTER 17

I t took the best part of two nights and the day in between before they had all finished the recces. They travelled back with Ahmad again scouting on foot ahead of the bikes. Jock and Geordie arrived at the RV and brought Shepherd and Jimbo up to date with everything they had done, then Jock and Geordie set to work scoping out the rest of the site.

Ahmad had managed to penetrate right to the centre of the operational area. He had waited to one side of the main gates, near a group of tents and barrack huts that had been thrown together in a shanty town settlement to house the temporary workers from the site. Just after dawn, he saw a large party of civilian workers emerge from their camp and head for the site to start their day's work and he had simply tagged on to the back of the group and walked straight past the disinterested-looking guards on the gates. He had then followed the workers towards the main construction site, within a natural cave in the side of the mountain.

He found an unattended wheelbarrow with a couple of sacks of cement in it, and trundled it down the trackway and into the cave, which the Iranians were excavating and extending to create a cavernous generator hall large enough to hold three huge turbine generators, at least one of which was already up and running. The generator hall was linked to an as yet only partially-built nuclear power area even deeper inside the mountain. By eavesdropping on the workers around him and talking to some of them, he discovered that the Iranians were using a workforce that had been shipped in from all over Iran, as well as a large contingent of unskilled labourers from Pakistan and India. Most of the activity was being carried out during the day with a reduced workforce continuing through the night, and the whole area was one vast construction site.

None of the workers he had talked to had actually worked in the nuclear area but the heavy military presence and the extremely high security surrounding the entrance to that part of the site – including a tunnel driven off the main chamber that was big enough to accommodate a jumbo jet and with massive armoured steel doors – suggested that what they were producing or planning to produce there was most unlikely to be just civil nuclear power.

'And in any case, as we all know,' Shepherd said, 'one of the by-products of civilian nuclear power stations using reactors like the old British Magnox ones, is uranium or plutonium that is capable of being enriched to make weapons grade material. One way or another, they're heading for a bomb.'

Although they spent some time discussing Ahmad's discoveries about the nuclear site, it was his comments about the excavation of the cavern itself that really made Shepherd's eyes light up. 'Some of the workers told me that they were frightened to work there,' Ahmad said, 'and they only stayed because their families back in Pakistan desperately needed the money. I assumed it was because of the risk from nuclear radiation, but it was not that at all. They told me they were afraid of roof falls. Some of them had heard the engineers talking, and because of doubts about the stability of the mountain, they were having to reinforce the interior of the whole excavation with steel beams and reinforced concrete.'

'Tell me about the heavy equipment they've got in there, Ahmad,' Shepard said.

'I saw diggers, tipper trucks, cherry pickers and mobile cranes.'

'And they were all kept within the cavern?'

'As far as I could tell.'

'And all self-propelled?'

'I think so, yes,' Ahmad said, looking puzzled.

Shepherd gave a broad smile. 'Excellent.'

When he had gleaned all the information that there was to be had, Ahmad had simply joined a group of workers heading back to their camp at the end of their shift. The guards were slightly more alert to those leaving the site than entering it, but their only concern seemed to be to prevent the workers from pilfering tools and materials, and they did not even glance at Ahmad's face as, empty-handed, he walked past them out of the site. He made as if to enter the camp with the other workers, but hung back for a few seconds as they dispersed among the tents and barrack huts and then slipped away into the desert and made his way to the RV with the others.

Jock had meanwhile put together a detailed sketch map of the defences of the site. They were made up for the main part by Russian-built ground-to-air missile systems and anti-aircraft guns. There were a number of SA-8 "Wasp" mobile systems that had four missile launch rails and an engagement radar, all mounted on the same six-wheeled armoured, amphibious truck. The Iranians also had SA-11 "Buk" missiles – medium range missiles, launched from a tracked vehicle and designed to counter Cruise missiles, smart bombs and unmanned drones as well as fast-jets – and SA-13 "Gophers": mobile tracked launchers of eight, short-range, low-altitude missiles with infra-red guidance systems, intended to counter the threat from attack helicopters and aircraft attacking at low-level.

The missile batteries were also supported by ZU-23–2 "Sergeis", ground-mounted, twin-barrelled, 23-millimetre auto-cannons. They had such a terrifying rate of fire – 400 to 2000 rounds per minute – that they were feared even more than missiles by low flying aircrew, because although they had electronic counter-measures that offered some protection against missiles, no electronic protection had ever been devised that could divert a cannon shell from its track.

Some of the cannons were mounted on flat-bed trucks to give them mobility, while others were sited in fixed positions, giving the whole area an inter-locking air defence system.

The anti-aircraft sites were manned by elite Republican Guard units but the guards patrolling the perimeter and controlling access to the site were drawn from low grade, conscript infantry troops.

'It seems to me that the Iranian authorities are relying on the remoteness of the location for their security,' Jock said. 'They appear to be concentrating on the threat of an air strike and have discounted any possibility of a ground attack. They're so busy scanning the skies for Israeli or Saudi jets that they can't see what's in front of their noses.'

Geordie had infiltrated the administrative area used by the engineers working on the site and the military area housing both guard forces. 'The engineers appeared to be construction experts or connected to the nuclear installation,' he said, 'but it was difficult to differentiate between the two, because they all dressed in the same white overalls and the writing on their vehicles was so stylised that it was impossible to read.'

'Impossible for an uneducated Geordie, anyway,' Jock said, never able to resist the chance of a dig at his best mate.

Geordie ignored the interruption. 'The army garrison are equipped mainly with wheeled Armoured Personnel Carriers, BTR-60s and BRDM Scout Cars with some Russian jeeps and trucks thrown in. I managed to get close to the Officers' Mess in the camp briefly and I identified the UAZ belonging to Farehdi. I was that close I could have booby-trapped it while I was there if I'd had the right kit.'

'Bloody good job you didn't though,' Shepherd said. 'I've got other plans for that bastard. Anyway, great work guys. I think we're good to go. So, detailed tasks: Ahmad and I will lead the attack inside the mountain. Ahmad, you'll be taking on targets at ground level while I attempt to quite literally bring the house down around us. Jock and Geordie, your task is to take over one of the ZU-23–2 sites that overlook the cave entrance so you can use it to provide cover for Ahmad and me. Once you are in control of it, Jock, you can man the weapon solo while Geordie detaches himself and takes on targets of opportunity among the civilian engineers and crucially, steals Farehdi's jeep.

'This last part is critical, if we are going to persuade Farehdi to make one final rash act. Remember: know your enemy. Farehdi is an arrogant bastard and he will be incensed that we have got the better of him several times. If we get this right, he will follow us practically anywhere to try and get his revenge, and once we have got him back here, leading him into the ambush that Jimbo has been working on, he'll find he has bitten off a lot more than he can chew. And speaking of that reminds me, Geordie, take a wrench with you and when you've got your hands on Farehdi's UAZ, use it to turn the front hubs to engage four-wheel-drive. The Western manuals will tell you that you can engage four-wheel-drive on it by using the gear stick, but that is absolute bollocks, you have to do it manually, using a wrench. Trust me, I was caught out that way on an earlier operation and I was lucky to escape with my life.'

They spent some time sketching out a scale plan of the target area, including the size, initiation type and placement points for the explosive charges that Shepherd and the others would be laying, together with the routes they would take in and out of the site, and the location of the pieces of engineering equipment that would be vital to the success of the mission. They then painstakingly assembled, prepared and tested every possible item they would need at the target. The more that could be done away from the site, the less time they would have to spend in the danger zone on target.

As they continued their preparations, Ahmad was intrigued when he saw Geordie slipping explosive initiation sets inside some of the condoms from the air-drop. Geordie held one up for him to inspect. 'Rubber perishes quite rapidly in contact with petrol,' Geordie explained. 'So if I put the initiation set inside one of these johnnies and then drop it inside a vehicle fuel tank, eventually the petrol will rot away the rubber and the set will initiate. And because it's floating on the surface of the fuel, it'll go off in the fuel/air space at the top of the tank, causing an explosion. Petrol is surprisingly difficult to ignite without sufficient oxygen so if the initiator was under the fuel at the bottom of the tank, it probably wouldn't go bang because of the lack of oxygen. One other factor that makes these particularly useful is that they will go off entirely at random, without any advance warning or visible cause. So as soon as one or two have gone "Bang!" the whole of the rest of the fleet of drivers will be terrified to get behind a wheel, in case their vehicle is next. All good psychological terror games, don't you think?'

Finally, everything was ready. The equipment had all been assembled, checked and re-checked, the charges prepared and carefully packed, and they had loaded themselves down with maximum ammunition. They had decided on a last light entry to the target, during the change-over between the day and night shifts working in the cave, when there would be the maximum amount of human traffic coming on and off site.

Now the waiting was at last nearly over, everybody felt a huge sense of relief. Whether it was a success or a failure, whether they lived or died, anything was better than the gnawing uncertainty of the long wait before the attack could be launched.

CHAPTER 18

In the gathering dusk they headed west into the setting sun, communicating with each other by clicks on their radios, heard in their ear-pieces. Each pre-arranged group of clicks meant the same to the sender and receiver, and that cut down greatly on the amount of time the team were on the air, making it harder for any Iranians to intercept their communications.

They travelled in two separate groups, Ahmad and Shepherd riding their bikes together while Jock and Geordie went by a different route. They cached their bikes in cover a mile or so from the site and walked into the target from there, and by last light both groups were in position and ready to begin the assault.

Jock and Geordie took over the ZSU site with the minimum of fuss and noise. The four-man gun crew had been on duty for several days without relief, and were tired and lethargic. Two men were asleep, the others dozing over their weapon, and none of them saw the two figures creeping towards them in the darkness. The first hint of danger was also the last sensation they would ever experience as the two men at the weapon were taken out in a flurry of silent knife and killer blows. The two who had been asleep had no warning at all; their throats were cut, each with a powerful hand clamped over their mouth as their lifeblood pumped away.

Jock wiped his knife on the sleeve of one of the dead men, dragged the bodies clear of the weapon and then swung the twin barrels of the cannon to cover the entrance to the cave. He then radioed Shepherd and gave the clicked signal that told him all was now clear for the main assault. As he did so, Geordie slipped away into the darkness.

As soon as Shepherd heard the clicks from Jock in his earpiece, he and Ahmad rose from cover and headed into the target area, making their slow way through the tide of workmen leaving the work-site, tired and hungry after a long hard shift. Shepherd was pushing a wooden handcart liberated from the workers' camp, which contained their ops kit and explosives, while Ahmad walked ahead of him, clearing a path through the resentful workers. As Ahmad had told him, the security was almost non-existent, just a couple of disinterested guards who were preoccupied in casting their eyes over the departing throng, checking to see if they were taking anything of value off the site. No one gave Shepherd or Ahmad a second look.

Shepherd and Ahmad kept their heads down as they walked by the sentries and made their way into the cave. But as soon as they were inside they were accosted by a man whose clothing and attitude marked him out as a supervisor. Speaking in Farsi, he demanded to see what was in the barrow. Ahmad began to mumble a vague reply, playing for time, until Shepherd could cut the conversation short by dropping the supervisor with a vicious blow to the head, laying him out flat in the dirt. He shot a quick glance around but the other workers were preoccupied with their own tasks and had seen nothing, so he dragged the unconscious supervisor behind a parked digger and then trundled the barrow across to one of the self-propelled cherry-pickers Ahmad had seen on his intelligence gathering mission. It was parked against one of the cave walls and Shepherd transferred his kit to the hopper.

Having made sure that Shepherd had reached the cherry-picker safely, Ahmad ran across to the area where the first of the three electricity generating turbines was quietly humming. As he had rehearsed with Shepherd, he placed a standard charge in the "elephants arse": the orifice where the shaft exited from the turbine. He repeated the procedure twice more with the other two turbines. When the charges detonated, they would warp the shaft and bearings and the spinning shafts would then cause the machines to shake themselves to bits. He then moved to the entrance and took up a guard position to prevent reinforcements entering the cave.

Meanwhile Shepherd was steering the cherry picker to the centre of the cave, raising the hopper up to roof height. The ceiling was about forty feet above the uneven floor of the cave and the hopper was bouncing about wildly, but Shepherd kept a firm grip and was soon in position to begin placing his charges in a linear pattern between the steel I-beams and the rough rock roof of the cave. He worked quickly, ignored by the workers elsewhere in the cave, and had only two more charges to place when there was a sudden burst of fire below him. Looking down he saw a couple of sections of smartly dressed Iranian troops engaging Ahmad with automatic fire.

They seemed professional which suggested they were the site quick reaction force, Republican Guards or more likely airborne troops from the look of them. The Iranians were as yet oblivious to Shepherd's presence above them and he quickly finished tying off the last of his charges. At almost the same moment, Ahmad took a shot in the shoulder, but even though he was seriously wounded, he continued to engage the enemy, loosing off brief bursts of fire using his good arm that kept them pinned down near the entrance.

With a choice of initiation timer sets to choose from, ranging from instantaneous to fifteen minutes, Shepherd changed plans and, instead of a longer timer, activated the one that would detonate the charges in ninety seconds. He then started to take out the Iranian soldiers, firing one handed with his AK-47, while at the same time lowering the hopper closer to the ground.

The Iranians returned fire but the steel bucket of the hopper deflected many of the rounds, sending the ricochets whining away into the far reaches of the cave and causing fresh panic among the night-shift workers, most of whom had flung themselves flat in the dirt as soon as the firing started and then wormed their way into whatever shelter they could find among the machinery and equipment.

Without waiting for the hopper to complete its descent to the floor of the cave, Shepherd jumped the last ten feet, diving and rolling quickly before getting up and continuing the firefight with the enemy troops, who were now beginning to pull back in some disarray.

Shepherd continued to loose off short bursts of accurate fire while working his way towards Ahmad, who was still firing away.

In the midst of the chaos of the battle, Shepherd heard the clicks in his earpiece that signalled that Geordie had reached the RV point with their transport. Barely pausing, Shepherd clicked a signal to Jock, alerting him not to fire on them as they exited the cave, then tossed a grenade towards the Iranian troops. As it erupted in a blinding flash of white phosphorus, he broke cover, scooped up the protesting Ahmad and slung him over his shoulder, then sprinted for the cave mouth. A few Iranian rounds whined past his ears and struck sparks from the rock walls of the cave, but he kept running, dodging and weaving as he went, to throw off their aim.

As soon as he emerged from the cave mouth, he became aware of the thunderous clatter of the 23-millimetre cannon. Jock was still keeping himself busy, shooting up the Iranian troops and the other cannon and missile launchers ranged around the site.

Shepherd had barely got into the open, still with Ahmad on his shoulders, when there was a muffled explosion from behind them, and they were engulfed in a cloud of dust and smoke. Glancing back, he saw the top of the mountain beginning to implode. The ninety-second initiation sets had done their work and tens of thousands of tons of rock were now collapsing, crushing and burying the embryonic nuclear facility beyond any hope of repair. Fragments of rock and debris fell around Shepherd as he ran and the roiling cloud of dust still engulfed him, giving him some additional cover from the Iranian guns.

Still carrying Ahmad over his shoulder, he ran on through the slowly clearing fog of dust and when they reached the pick-up point, they were greeted by a grinning Geordie, sitting in the pristine UAZ jeep, complete with the pennant on the bonnet and the white covers on the seats. There was no doubt the vehicle was Farehdi's pride and joy. Shepherd lowered Ahmad onto the back seat, where the blood from his shoulder wound at once began to stain the white fabric. Shepherd jumped in alongside him and fired a few more bursts at the dwindling number of

Iranian troops who were still trying to engage them, as Geordie gunned the engine and sent the jeep careering across the site towards the entrance.

Whether the guards on the gate thought it was Farehdi himself making his customary escape from danger, or were simply too terrified to think anything, not a shot was fired at the jeep as they roared through the gates. Geordie span the wheel and screeched to a halt a hundred metres farther on. There was a pause as Jock fired off one final prolonged burst with the 23-millimetre cannon before he abandoned the weapon. There was the sound of running footsteps in the dark and Jock suddenly appeared, grinning hugely. He clambered in alongside them. 'There's fuck all left back there,' he said. 'Let's get out of here.'

'And let's make plenty of noise while we're doing so,' Shepherd said. 'We want them to be certain that they'll know where to find us so that Farehdi gives chase.'

They drove off at high speed, shooting flares into the air and dropping grenades behind them as they went, roaring away into the heart of the desert.

'Result boys!' Shepherd said, when he could make himself heard above the whoops from the other two. 'That must have put their programme back several years. It won't stop them altogether, but it will give our side a pretty healthy breathing space to see if they can find another way of tackling the problem.'

Geordie, the patrol medic, halted for an instant and swapped places with Shepherd. While Shepherd drove on, Geordie, doing his best to ignore the jolting of the jeep, tended to Ahmad's wound, cleaning and dressing it and making him as comfortable as he possibly could. 'I've no drip or saline till we get back to where we stashed the rest of our kit,' Geordie said, 'but don't worry, Ahmad, I've never lost a patient yet if he was breathing when I got to him.' He paused. 'Although I suppose there's always a first time.' He waited a few beats of silence before adding 'Only joking mate, you're going to be all right.'

CHAPTER 19

Colonel Farehdi stood looking out of the turret of his BRDM armoured scout car at a plume of black smoke rising from the desert in the distance ahead of him. His was the lead vehicle at the head of a hastily assembled column of armoured personnel carriers and fuel bowsers. His scout car was festooned with an array of radio aerials, and Farehdi was constantly in touch with the other vehicle commanders, berating them for being too cautious and not keeping pace with his vehicle. Farehdi had seen his career and future prospects evaporate in a few short minutes and he was determined to exact at least a measure of revenge.

He urged the column forward again, only ordering his own driver to slow his pace as they were approaching the source of the smoke. It was hidden for the moment, just beyond a low bluff where the track passed between two rock outcrops rising from the desert floor. A series of soft sand-dunes flanked them, making the track the only way forward for a vehicle. It was an obvious place for an ambush and

Farehdi at once held up his hand, halting the column. He snapped an order at one of the two gunners, the other members of the scout car's crew. 'Climb to the top of that outcrop and look for signs of the enemy. They may be lying in wait.'

The soldier's face revealed his concern at what this task might bring down on him, but seeing his hesitation, Farehdi unleashed a furious, obscenity-strewn tirade at him, calling him dog, coward, son of a whore and worse. The soldier's fear of his commander overcame his fear of what might be waiting for him beyond the ridge and he almost fell from the scout car in his desperation to escape Farehdi. The Colonel kept a baleful watch from the turret as the soldier made his hesitant, fearful way up the outcrop, pausing every couple of paces, despite fresh tirades of abuse from Farehdi, to peer suspiciously at every rock and thorn bush before moving on. When he neared the ridgeline, he slowed even more, dropping to his hands and knees and then belly-crawling the last few metres to the top of the outcrop. He lay in the dirt for a few moments, gathering his nerve, then slowly raised his head and put his binoculars to his eyes, raking the desert beyond the ridge with his eyes. He remained motionless there for two minutes, then got to his feet, waved his arms over his head and hurried back down the slope to the waiting scout car.

'The smoke is from a burning vehicle, Colonel,' he said in Farsi. 'There are no other vehicles in sight and no sign of the enemy soldiers.'

'What vehicle is on fire?'

The soldier hesitated for a fraction of a second. 'It was impossible to tell, Sir,' he said, too frightened to tell Farehdi the truth. 'It was too burnt and blackened.'

If he had been hoping for an acknowledgment of his courage in exposing himself to potential enemy fire, he was to be disappointed. Farehdi merely grunted, flicked his hand in a dismissive gesture to send the gunner back to his position, then signalled to the rest of the column to move out after him.

His still burning rage reached white heat when his scout car breasted the summit of the track as it passed between the rock outcrops and he could see the burning vehicle ahead of him. As he drew closer to it, he realised that the column of smoke was belching from what remained of his beloved UAZ, abandoned by the SAS men in the middle of the track and then torched. Still burning fiercely, it was now little more than a heap of blackened, twisted metal, with the pennant that had once flown proudly from the bonnet, now dangling from a snapped off radio aerial stuck into the side of a nearby sand dune.

Farehdi again held up a hand to signal the column to halt and, reluctant to trust his gunner's report, he scanned the terrain through his binoculars, searching for any sign that the soldiers who had destroyed his vehicle were still there, lying in wait for him. After five minutes of careful scrutiny, he was confident that the desert around the burning vehicle was empty of life. The enemy soldiers must have fled. More angry than relieved at that, he waved the column forward again, determined to pick up the enemies' tracks, pursue them and run them to ground. He wanted them captured alive and he vowed to himself that they would be begging for death, long before he had finished with them.

He radioed another order to his commanders. 'The area is clear of enemy troops. Secure a perimeter, mount guards and then send out patrols at once to search for tracks. Those foreign devils must be found.'

As the scout car nosed past the burning wreckage of the other vehicle, Farehdi leaned further out of the turret, peering at what was left of his UAZ. As he did so, he glimpsed a flash from the corner of his eye and heard a double explosion as an RPG fired at the scout car blew off one of its drive wheels. Already off-balance, he was thrown sideways and the turret's metal rim bit into his hip as he was sent flying over it. His fingers scrabbled in vain for any grip on the armoured flank of the scout car and he crashed to the ground as the vehicle lurched to one side and ground to a halt, it's wheel-less rear wing tilted downwards and gouging a furrow in the sand and rock.

At the same instant as the RPG round detonated, there was a massive explosion from beneath the rearmost vehicle of the convoy, throwing it high into the air. Instantaneous panic spread through the column as fresh explosions and RPG rounds erupted around them. The occupants of the other vehicles, battened down behind their armour-plating, and barely able to see or breathe, were convinced that they were surrounded and being shelled to pieces by artillery. The restricted view from inside the armoured personnel carriers made it impossible to see from where the incoming fire was emanating and what had been a reasonably disciplined force was transformed in seconds into a rabble. The driver of each vehicle fought to reach what he thought was safety, and since no two drivers had the same thought, the result was chaos. Some turned left, some right, some tried to turn round and back-track while others tried to race forward. There were crashes and collisions which only added to the chaos and confusion.

Other drivers stuck rigidly to the tracks of the vehicles in front of them, thinking that this would keep them safe from mines, only to be shredded and vaporised by the molten metal blasted upwards by the detonation of an anti-tank mine with a ratchet fuse that had allowed the first few vehicles to pass before destroying the next. Whichever way Farehdi's men tried to turn, they were met by yet more explosions, while the air was filled with the whine of shrapnel from exploding grenades. More vehicles were blown up and two fuel bowsers exploded when one of the Iranian armoured personnel carriers crashed into them. Burning fuel sprayed in all directions, igniting the thorn bushes and scrub.

The area ambush painstakingly designed by Shepherd and meticulously built by Jimbo, worked exactly as planned. Every placement of a mine had been carefully calculated, necklaces of grenades had been aligned to scatter shrapnel where it would cause most damage, and all the explosions had been calculated to look and sound like the product of artillery fire. Even more crucially, once the stream of orders from the head of the Iranian force had been silenced, all order and reason had vanished from his men. Farehdi had never encouraged them to think for themselves, only to blindly follow whatever orders he issued. When he was no longer in a position to give those orders, they were helpless. Know Your Enemy had been vindicated.

The firing continued as the SAS men extinguished the last feeble sparks of resistance from the column. The wisps of black smoke still drifting up from the original fire in the remains of Farehdi's UAZ were now lost among the pall of dust and smoke from a dozen destroyed armoured personnel carriers, scout cars and fuel bowsers.

When the last rounds had been fired, to be greeted only with an answering silence, Shepherd levered himself up out of his fox-hole, no more than fifty yards from the Iranian's immobilised BRDM scout car. By now the usually impeccable colonel was covered in dust from the blasts around him. Battered, dazed and wounded, he was a shadow of his formerly irascible self. He was leaning against the side of his vehicle, barely able to stand upright.

Shepherd was undecided about what to do with him. One choice was to take him prisoner and transport him back with them to Pakistan for interrogation but, valuable though his information would be, Farehdi would inevitably slow them up and add substantially to the risk of compromise as they exfiltrated. The other option was simply to kill him out of hand and cleanse the earth of a truly evil man.

While Shepherd was going through the thought processes, he became aware of Ahmad pushing past him, muttering to himself. At first Shepherd thought Ahmad was just delirious from his wound as he stumbled towards Farehdi, but then he saw Ahmad's uninjured arm snake around the Iranian officer and embrace him to his chest in an unbreakable clasp.

'He's got a grenade!' shouted Geordie.

Shepherd shouted 'No, Ahmad!' and started to run towards him, but then threw himself full-length in the dirt as he heard Ahmad's last words: 'This is for Massoud.' Ahmad bit down on the pin and pulled it from the grenade and seconds later there was a deafening blast. Shepherd heard shrapnel whining over his heads and a spattering sound, like raindrops, as softer fragments fell around him. When he got to his feet, there was nothing left of the two men, except for some bloody fragments of clothing and pieces of blackened flesh, and one of Farehdi's boots from which part of his leg was still protruding.

Jock's hand gripped Shepherd's shoulder. 'Why the hell do they do that?' he asked. 'Kill themselves to take out an enemy?'

'I don't know,' said Shepherd quietly.

'It makes no bloody sense,' said Geordie, joining them.

'It made sense to Ahmad, I guess,' said Shepherd. 'At least he got his revenge.'

'But where does that come from?' asked Jock. 'The idea that it's worth killing yourself if it kills your enemy? I mean, sure, I'd die for the people I love, but in combat, there's no way I'd take on a suicide mission.'

Shepherd nodded. 'I hear what you're saying, Jock. You always want a fighting chance.'

'Hundreds of thousands died in the trenches,' said Geordie.

'That's different,' said Jock. 'At least they were fighting. What Ahmad did – it was suicide, pure and simple. What was going through his mind? He gets to kill the man who killed his uncle, I get that. But he killed himself to kill Farehdi.' He shook his head. 'It makes no sense to me. If someone killed someone close to me, then damn right I'd want them dead. But I wouldn't top myself in the process.'

'Maybe he believed in Heaven,' said Shepherd. 'Maybe he believed that killing himself for a noble cause means he goes to Heaven. Same as the guys in the planes on 9–11.'

'Yeah? He gets to live with Allah, is that it?' Jock sneered. 'That's nonsense and we all know it.'

'It doesn't matter if what he believes is true or not,' said Shepherd. 'What matters is whether or not he believes in it, and he obviously did. You saw the way he died. There was no doubt, no hesitation, he just did it and did it happily. I'm just glad that he was on our side and it wasn't one of us he wanted to kill. We're trained to fight soldiers, men who fight by the same rules we follow, and one of those rules is that you go into any combat situation expecting to come out of it alive. But if we come up against an enemy who will quite happily die if it means we die too...' He shrugged. 'I've no idea how you fight an enemy like that.'

'Let's hope we never have to,' said Jock. He grinned. 'Inshallah.'

About the Author

Stephen Leather is one of the UK's most successful thriller writers, an eBook and *Sunday Times* bestseller and author of the critically acclaimed Dan "Spider' Shepherd series and the Jack Nightingale supernatural detective novels. Before becoming a novelist he was a journalist for more than ten years on newspapers such as *The Times,* the *Daily Mirror,* the *Glasgow Herald,* the *Daily Mail* and the *South China Morning Post* in Hong Kong. He is one of the country's most successful eBook authors and his eBooks have topped the Amazon Kindle charts in the UK and the US. *The Bookseller* magazine named him as one of the 100 most influential people in the UK publishing world. Amazon has identified him as one of their Top 10 independent self-publishers. His book *The Basement* is one of Amazon's most successful self-published titles of all time. Born in Manchester, he began writing full-time in 1992. His bestsellers have been translated into fifteen languages. He has also written for television shows such as London's Burning, The Knock and the BBC's Murder in Mind series and two of his books, *The Stretch* and *The Bombmaker*, were filmed for TV.

To find out more, you can visit his website at www.stephenleather.com, or find him on Facebook at Stephen Leather Author.

DARK FORCES

Hodder and Stoughton have published twelve books featuring Dan 'Spider' Shepherd written by Sunday Times bestselling author Stephen Leather. The thirteenth, Dark Forces, is now available to buy from Amazon and other retailers.

When you're caught between two evils, only the most decisive will survive. The thirteenth book in action supremo Stephen Leather's Spider Shepherd series is his most pulse-pounding yet.

A violent South London gang will be destroyed if Dan 'Spider' Shepherd can gather enough evidence against them while posing as a ruthless hitman. What he doesn't know is that his work as an undercover agent for MI5 is about to intersect with the biggest terrorist operation ever carried out on British soil.

Only weeks before, Shepherd witnessed a highly skilled IS sniper escape from a targeted missile strike in Syria. But never in his wildest dreams did he expect to come across the shooter next in a grimy East London flat.

Spider's going to have to proceed with extreme caution if he is to prevent the death of hundreds of people, but at the same time, when the crucial moment comes he will have to act decisively. The clock is ticking and only he stands between us and Armageddon....

Here is a taster of the book:

DARK FORCES
by Stephen Leather

The man's name was Mohammed al-Hussain, a common enough name in Syria. But the Mohammed al-Hussain lying prone on the roof of the two-storey building was no ordinary man. He was a sniper, one of the best in the world. He had 256 kills to his credit, each one meticulously recorded in the small cloth-bound notebook he kept in his back pocket. Each entry detailed the nature of the target, the location and the distance. Almost all of his kills were Syrian government soldiers.

He was twenty-two years old, his skin the colour of weak coffee with plenty of milk. He had soft brown eyes that belonged more to a lovesick spaniel than the tried and tested assassin he was. His beard was long and bushy but his nails were neatly clipped and glistened as if they had been varnished. Around his head was a knotted black scarf with the white insignia of Islamic State, the caliphate that claimed authority over all Muslims around the world. His weapon was lying on a sandbag.

When he had first started sniping, he had used a Russian-made Dragunov SVD rifle, accurate up to six hundred metres. It was a lightweight and reliable weapon, capable of semi-automatic fire and equipped with a ten-round magazine. Most of his kills back then had been at around two hundred metres. His commander had spotted his skill with the weapon and had recommended him for specialist training. He was pulled off the front line and spent four weeks in the desert at a remote training camp.

There, he was introduced to the British L115A3 sniper rifle. It was the weapon of choice for snipers in the British SAS and the American Delta Force, and it hadn't taken al-Hussain long to appreciate its advantages. It had been designed by Olympic target shooters and fired an 8.59mm round, the extra weight resulting in less deflection over long ranges. In fact, in the right hands the L115A3 could hit a human-sized target at 1,400 metres, and even at that distance the round would do more damage than a magnum bullet at close range.

The L115A3 was fitted with a suppressor to cut down the flash and noise it made. No one killed by a bullet from his L115A3 ever heard it coming. It was the perfect rifle for carrying around – it weighed less than seven kilograms and had a folding stock so it could easily be slid into a backpack.

It had an adjustable cheek-piece so that the marksman's eye could be comfortably aligned with the Schmidt & Bender 25 x magnification scope. Al-Hussain put his eye to it now and made a slight adjustment to the focus. His target was a house just over a thousand metres away. It was home to the mother of a colonel in the Syrian Army, and today was her birthday. The colonel was a good son and, at just after eight o'clock, had arrived at the house to have breakfast with his mother. Fifteen minutes later, al-Hussain had taken up position on the roof. The colonel was a prime target and had been for the best part of a year.

The L115A3 cost thirty-five thousand dollars in the United States but more than double that in the Middle East. The Islamic State was careful who it gave the weapons to, but al-Hussain was an obvious choice. His notepad confirmed the benefits of using the British rifle. His kills went from an average of close to two hundred metres with the Dragunov to more than eight hundred. His kill rate increased too. With the Dragunov he averaged three kills a day on active service. With the L115A3, more often than not he recorded at least five. The magazine held only five shells but that was enough. Firing more than two shots in succession was likely to lead to his location being pinpointed. One was best. One shot, one kill. Then wait at least a few minutes before firing again. But al-Hussain wasn't planning on shooting more than once. There were two SUVs outside the mother's house and the soldiers had formed a perimeter around the building but the only target the sniper was interested in was the colonel.

'Are we good to go?' asked the man to the sniper's right. He was Asian, bearded, with a crooked hooked nose, and spoke with an English accent. He was one of thousands of foreign jihadists who had crossed the border into Syria to fight alongside Islamic State. The other man, the one to the sniper's left, was an Iraqi, darker-skinned and wearing glasses.

Al-Hussain spoke good English. His parents had sent him to one of the best schools in Damascus, International School of Choueifat. The school had an indoor heated pool, a gymnasium, a grass football pitch, a 400-metre athletics track, basketball and tennis courts. Al-Hussain had been an able pupil and had made full use of the school's sporting facilities.

Everything had changed when he had turned seventeen. Teenagers who had painted revolutionary slogans on a school wall had been arrested and tortured in the southern city of Deraa and thousands of people took to the streets to protest. The Syrian Army reacted by shooting the unarmed protesters, and by the summer of 2011 the protests had spread across the country. Al-Hussain had seen, first hand, the brutality of the government response. He saw his fellow students take up arms to defend themselves and at first he resisted, believing that peaceful protests would succeed eventually. He was wrong. The protests escalated and the country descended into civil war. What had been touted as an Arab Spring became a violent struggle as rebel brigades laid siege to government-controlled cities and towns, determined to end the reign of President Assad.

By the summer of 2013 more than a hundred thousand people had been killed and fighting had reached the capital, Damascus. In August of that year the Syrian government had killed hundreds of people on the outskirts of Damascus when they launched rockets filled with the nerve gas Sarin.

Al-Hussain's parents decided they had had enough. They closed their house in Mezze and fled to Lebanon with their two daughters, begging Mohammed to go with them. He refused, telling them he had to stay and fight for his country. As his family fled, al-Hussain began killing with a vengeance. He knew that the struggle was no longer just about removing President Assad. It was a full-blown war in which there could be only one victor.

Syria had been run by the president's Shia Alawite sect, but the country's Sunni majority had been the underdogs for a long time and wanted nothing less than complete control. Russia and Iran wanted President Assad to continue running the country, as did Lebanon. Together they poured billions of dollars into supporting the regime, while the US, the UK and France, along with Turkey, Saudi Arabia, Qatar and the rest of the Arab states, supported the Sunni-dominated opposition.

After the nerve gas attack, al-Hussain's unit switched their allegiance to Islamic State, which had been formed from the rump of al-Qaeda's operations in Iraq. Led by Abu Bakr al-Baghdadi, Islamic State had attracted thousands of foreign jihadists, lured by its promise to create an Islamic emirate from large chunks of Syria and Iraq. Islamic State grew quickly, funded in part by captured oilfields, taking first the provincial Syrian city of Raqqa and the Sunni city of Fallujah, in the western Iraqi province of Anbar.

As Islamic State grew, Mohammed al-Hussain was given ever more strategic targets. He was known as the sniper who never missed, and his notebook was filled with the names of high-ranking Syrian officers and politicians.

'He's coming out,' said the Brit, but al-Hussain had already seen the front door open. The soldiers outside started moving, scanning the area for potential threats. Al-Hussain put his eye to the scope and began to control his breathing. Slow and even. There was ten feet between the door and the colonel's SUV. A couple of seconds. More than enough time for an expert sniper like al-Hussain.

A figure appeared at the doorway and al-Hussain held his breath. His finger tightened on the trigger. It was important to squeeze, not pull. He saw a headscarf. The mother. He started breathing again, but slowly and tidally. She had her head against the colonel's chest. He was hugging her. The door opened wider.

She stepped back. He saw the green of the colonel's uniform. He held his breath. Tightened his finger.

The phone in the breast pocket of his jacket buzzed. Al-Hussain leaped to his feet, clasped the rifle to his chest and headed across the roof. The two spotters looked up at him, their mouths open. 'Run!' he shouted, but they stayed where they were. He didn't shout again. He concentrated on running at full speed to the stairwell. He reached the top and hurtled down the stone stairs. Just as he reached the ground floor a 45-kilogram Hellfire missile hit the roof at just under a thousand miles an hour.

Dan 'Spider' Shepherd stared at the screen. All he could see was whirling brown dust where once there had been a two-storey building. 'Did we get them all?' he asked.

Two airmen were sitting in front of him in high-backed beige leather chairs. They had control panels and joysticks in front of them and between them was a panel with two white telephones.

'Maybe,' said the man in the left-hand seat. He was Steve Morris, the flying officer in command, in his early forties with greying hair. Sitting next to him was Pilot Officer Denis Donoghue, in his thirties with ginger hair, cut short. 'What do you think, Denis?'

'The sniper was moving just before it hit. If he was quick enough he might have made it out. We got your two guys, guaranteed. Don't think they knew what hit them.'

'What about IR?' asked Shepherd.

Donoghue reached out and clicked a switch. The image on the main screen changed to a greenish hue. They could just about make out the ruins of the building. 'Not much help, I'm afraid,' said Donoghue. 'There isn't a lot left when you get a direct hit from a Hellfire.'

'Can we scan the surrounding area?'

Morris turned his joystick to the right. 'No problem,' he said. The drone banked to the right and so did the picture on the main screen in the middle of the display. The two screens to the left of it showed satellite images and maps, and above them was a tracker screen that indicated the location of the Predator. Below that was the head-up display that showed a radar ground image. But they were all staring at the main screen. Donoghue pulled the camera back, giving them a wider view of the area, still using the infrared camera.

The drone was an MQ-9, better known as the Predator B. Hunter-killer, built by General Atomics Aeronautical Systems at a cost of close to $17 million. It had a twenty-metre wingspan, a maximum speed of 300 m.p.h. and a range of a little more than a thousand miles. It could fly loaded for fourteen hours up to a height of fifteen thousand metres, carrying four Hellfire air-to-surface missiles and two Paveway laser-guided bombs.

One of the Hellfires had taken out the building, specifically an AGM-114P Hellfire II, specially designed to be fired from a high-altitude drone.

The Hellfire air-to-surface missile was developed for tank-hunting and the nickname came from its initial designation of Helicopter Launched, Fire and Forget Missile. But the armed forces of the West soon realised that, when fired from a high-flying drone, the Hellfire could be a potent assassination tool for taking out high-value targets. It was the Israelis who had first used it against an individual when their air force killed Hamas leader Ahmed Yassin in 2004. But the Americans and British had takethe technique to a whole new level, using it to great effect in Pakistan, Somalia, Iraq and Syria. Among the terrorists killed by Hellfire missiles launched from drones were Al-Shabaab leader Ahmad Abdi Godane, and British-born Islamic State terrorist Mohammed Emwazi, also known as Jihadi John.

The Hellfire missile was efficient and, at less than a hundred thousand dollars a shot, cost-effective. It was just over five feet long, had a range of eight thousand metres and carried a nine-kilogram shaped charge that was more than capable of taking out a tank. It was, however, less effective against a stone building. While there was no doubt that the men on the roof would have died instantly, the sniper might well have survived, if he had made it outside.

Shepherd twisted in his seat. Alex Shaw, the mission coordinator, was sitting at his desk in front of six flat-screen monitors. He was in his early thirties with a receding hairline and wire-framed spectacles. 'What do you think, Alex? Did we get him?'

'I'd love to say yes, Spider, but there's no doubt he was moving.' He shrugged. 'He could have got downstairs and out before the missile hit but he'd have to have been moving fast.'

Shepherd wrinkled his nose. The primary target had been a British jihadist, Ruhul Khan and it had been Khan they had spent four hours following until he had reached the roof. It was only when the sniper had unpacked his rifle that Shepherd realised what the men were up to. While the death of the British jihadist meant the operation had been a success, it was frustrating not to know if they'd succeeded in taking out the sniper.

Shaw stood up and stretched, then walked over to stand by Shepherd. Donoghue had switched the camera back to regular HD. There were several pick-up trucks racing away from the ruins of the building, and a dozen or so men running towards it. None of the men on the ground looked like the sniper. It was possible he'd made it to a truck, but unlikely. And if he had made it, there was no way of identifying him from the air.

'We'll hang around and wait for the smoke to clear,' said Shaw. 'They might pull out the bodies. Muslims like to bury their dead within twenty-four hours.' He took out a packet of cigarettes. 'Time for a quick smoke.'

'Just give me a minute or two, will you, Alex?' asked Shepherd. 'Let's see if we can work out what the sniper was aiming at.'

'No problem,' said Shaw, dropping back into his seat.

'Start at about three hundred metres and work out,' said Shepherd.

'Are you on it, Steve?' asked Shaw.

'Heading two-five-zero,' said Morris, slowly moving his joystick. 'What are we looking for?'

'Anything a sniper might be interested in,' said Shepherd. 'Military installation. Army patrol. Government building.'

'It's mainly residential,' said Donoghue, peering at the main screen.

Shepherd stared at the screen. Donoghue was right. The area was almost all middle-class homes, many with well-tended gardens. Finding out who the occupants were would be next to impossible, and there were dozens of houses within the sniper's range. There was movement at the top of the screen. Five vehicles, travellmoving fast. 'What's that?' he asked.

Donoghue changed the camera and zoomed in on the convoy. Two army jeeps in front of a black SUV with tinted windows, followed by an army truck with a heavy machine-gun mounted on the top followed by a troop-carrier. 'That's someone important, right enough,' said Donoghue.

Shepherd nodded. 'How far from where the sniper was?'

'A mile or so.' Donoghue wrinkled his nose. 'That's a bit far, isn't it?'

'Not for a good one,' said Shepherd. 'And he looked as if he knew what he was doing.' He pointed at the screen. 'They're probably running because of the explosion. Whoever that guy is, he'll probably never know how close he came to taking a bullet.'

'Or that HM Government saved his bacon,' said Shaw. He grinned. 'Well, not bacon, obviously.'

'Can we get back to the house, see if the smoke's cleared?' said Shepherd. He stood and went over to Shaw's station. 'Can you get me close-ups of the sniper and his gun?'

'No problem. It'll take a few minutes. I'm not sure how good the images will be.'

'We've got technical guys who can clean them up,' said Shepherd.

'Denis, could you handle that for our guest?' said Shaw, then to Shepherd: 'Thumb drive okay?'

'Perfect.'

'Put a selection of images on a thumb drive, Denis, while I pop out for a smoke.' Shaw pushed himself up out of his chair.

'I'm on it,' said Donoghue.

Shaw opened a door and Shepherd followed him out. The unit was based in a container, the same size and shape as the ones used to carry goods on ships. There were two in a large hangar. Both were a dull yellow, with rubber wheels at either end so that they could be moved around, and large air-conditioning units attached to keep the occupants cool. The hangar was at RAF Waddington, four miles south of the city of Lincoln.

Shaw headed for the hangar entrance as he lit a cigarette. On the wall by the door was the badge of 13th Squadron – a lynx's head in front of a dagger – and a motto: ADJUVAMUS TUENDO, 'We Assist by Watching'. It was something of a misnomer as the squadron did much more than watch. Shaw blew smoke at the mid-morning sky. 'It was like he had a sixth sense, wasn't it? The way that sniper moved.'

'Could he have heard the drone?'

Shaw flashed him an admonishing look. The men of 13th Squadron didn't refer to the Predators as drones. They were RPAs, remotely piloted aircraft. Shepherd supposed it was because without the word 'pilot' in there somewhere, they might be considered surplus to requirements. Shepherd grinned and corrected himself. 'RPA. Could he have heard the RPA?'

'Not at the height we were at,' said Shaw.

'Must have spotters then, I guess.'

'The two men with him were eyes on the target. They weren't checking the sky.'

'I meant other spotters. Somewhere else. In communication with him via radio or phone.'

'I didn't see any of them using phones or radios,' said Shaw.

'True,' said Shepherd. 'But he could have a phone set to vibrate. The phone vibrates, he grabs his gun and runs.'

'Without warning his pals?'

'He could have shouted as he ran. They froze. Bang.'

'Our target was one of the guys with him. The Brit. Why are you so concerned about the one that got away?'

'Usually snipers have just one spotter,' said Shepherd. 'Their job is to protect the sniper and help him by calling the wind and noting the shots. That guy had two. Plus it looks like there were more protecting him from a distance. That suggests to me he's a valuable Islamic State resource. One of their best snipers. If he got away, I'd like at least to have some intel on him.'

'The Brit who was with him. How long have you been on his tail?'

'Khan's been on our watch list since he entered Syria a year ago. He's been posting some very nasty stuff on Facebook and Twitter.'

'It was impressive the way you spotted him coming out of the mosque. I couldn't tell him apart from the other men there.'

'I'm good at recognising people, close up and from a distance.'

'No question of that. I thought we were wasting our time when he got in that truck but then they picked up the sniper and went up on the roof. Kudos. But how did you spot him?'

'Face partly. I'd seen his file in London and I never forget a face. But I can recognise body shapes too, the way people move, the way they hold them-selves. That was more how I spotted Khan.'

'And what is he? British-born Asian who got radicalised?'

'In a nutshell,' said Shepherd. 'A year ago he was a computer-science student in Bradford. Dad's a doc-tor, a GP. Mum's a social worker. Go figure.'

'I don't understand it, do you? What the hell makes kids throw away their lives here and go to fight in the bloody desert?'

Shepherd shrugged. 'It's a form of brainwashing, if you ask me. Islamic State is a cult. And like any cult they can get their believers to do pretty much anything they want.'

Shaw blew smoke at the ground and watched it disperse in the wind. 'What sort of religion is it that says booze and bacon are bad things?' he said. 'How can anyone in their right mind believe for one moment that a God, any God, has a thing about alco-hol and pork? And that women should be kept cov-ered and shackled? And that old men should have sex with underage girls? It's fucking mad, isn't it?'

'I guess so. But it's not peculiar to Islam. Jews can't eat pork. Or seafood. And orthodox Jews won't work on the Sabbath.'

'Hey, I'm not singling out the Muslims,' said Shaw. 'It's all religions. We've got a Sikh guy in the regi-ment. , his name is, so you can imagine the ribbing he takes. Lovely guy. Bloody good airman. But he wears a turban, doesn't cut his hair and always has to have his ceremonial dagger on him. I've asked him, does he really believe God wants him not to cut his hair and to wear a silly hat?' Shaw grinned. 'Didn't use those exact words, obviously. He said, yeah, he believed it.' He took another pull on his cigarette. 'So here's the thing. Great guy. Great airman. A true professional. But if he really, truly, honestly believes that God wants him to grow his hair long, he's got mental-health issues. Seriously. He's as fucking mad as those nutters in the desert. If he truly believes God is telling him not to cut his hair, how do I know that one day his God won't tell him to pick up a rifle and blast away at non-believers? I don't, right? How the hell can you trust someone who allows a fictional entity to dictate their actions?'

'The world would be a much better place without religion –is that what you're saying?'

'I'm saying people should be allowed to believe in anything they want. Hell, there are still people who believe the earth is flat, despite all the evidence to the contrary. But the moment that belief starts to impact on others...' He shrugged. 'I don't know. I just want the world to be a nicer, friendlier place and it's not, and it feels to me it's religion that's doing the damage. That and sex.'

Shepherd smiled. 'Sex?'

'Haven't you noticed? The more relaxed a country is about sex, the less violent they are. The South Americans, they hardly ever go to war.'

'Argentina? The Falklands?'

'That was more of a misunderstanding than a war. But you know what I mean. If you're a young guy in Libya or Iraq or Pakistan, your chances of getting laid outside marriage are slim to none. They cover their women from head to toe, for a start. So all that male testosterone is swilling around with nowhere to go. Of course they're going to get ultra-violent.'

'So we should be sending hookers to Iraq and Libya, not troops?'

'I'm just saying, if these Islamic State guys got laid more often they wouldn't be going around chopping off so many heads. If Khan had been getting regular sex with a fit bird in Bradford, I doubt he'd be in such a rush to go fighting in the desert.'

'It's an interesting theory,' said Shepherd. 'But if I were you I'd keep it to myself.'

'Yeah, they took away our suggestions box years ago,' said Shaw. He flicked away the remains of his cigarette. 'I'll get you your thumb drive and you can be on your way.'

They went back inside the container. Donoghue had the thumb drive ready and handed it to Shepherd, who thanked him and studied the main screen. The dust and smoke had pretty much dispersed. The roof and upper floor had been reduced to rubble but the ground floor was still standing. 'No sign of any bodies?' asked Shepherd.

'Anything on the roof would have been vaporised, pretty much,' said Morris. 'If there was anyone on the ground floor, we won't know until they start clearing up, and at the moment that's not happening. They're keeping their distance. Probably afraid we'll let fly a second missile. We can hang around for a few hours but I won't be holding my breath.'

'Probably not worth it,' Shepherd said. 'Like you say, he's either vaporised or well out of the area.' He looked at his watch and flashed Shaw a tight smile. 'I've got to be somewhere, anyway.'

'A hot date?' asked Shaw.

'I wish,' said Shepherd. He couldn't tell Shaw he was heading off to kill someone and this time it was going to be up close and personal.

Dark Forces is available to buy now from Amazon and other retailers.

Made in the USA
Monee, IL
22 June 2021

71905669R10142